Lady Margaret Domvile

The King's Mother

Memoir of Margaret Beaufort, Countess of Richmond and Derby

Lady Margaret Domvile

The King's Mother
Memoir of Margaret Beaufort, Countess of Richmond and Derby

ISBN/EAN: 9783743398115

Manufactured in Europe, USA, Canada, Australia, Japa

Cover: Foto ©Raphael Reischuk / pixelio.de

Manufactured and distributed by brebook publishing software (www.brebook.com)

Lady Margaret Domvile

The King's Mother

THE
KING'S MOTHER.

MEMOIR OF MARGARET BEAUFORT,
COUNTESS OF RICHMOND AND DERBY.

BY

LADY MARGARET DOMVILE.

LONDON : BURNS & OATES, LIMITED.

1899.

BURNS AND OATES, LTD., PRINTERS, LONDON, W.

PREFACE.

SOME readers of Dr. Newman's "Apologia pro vita sua" may remember that, after recounting the circumstances under which the series of Lives of the English Saints was by him projected, and then dropped, the writer goes on to say that he is "glad of the opportunity of preserving what would otherwise be lost, the Catalogue of Saints I formed, which may be useful to others."

In this list, Dr. Newman tells us that he included "a few eminent, or holy persons, who, though not in the Sacred Catalogue, yet are recommended to our religious memory by their fame, learning, or by the benefits they have conferred on posterity ; these have been distinguished from the Saints by printing their names in italics." Their whole number is but fourteen, and the only woman's name so honoured is that of the Countess of Richmond.

Of this lady, the only complete and connected biography that has yet been published is one written by Miss Caroline Halsted,* to whose

---

* Brought out by Messrs. Smith and Elder in 1839.

previous essay on the subject the Directors of the Gresham Commemoration had awarded their annual premium. As the successful competitor, Miss Halsted was called on to publish her essay ; and it being, she tells us, her anxious desire to make the work as complete as possible, she examined attentively the Harleian, Cottonian, and Lansdowne MSS., and sought further information from many private and unpublished sources. To her painstaking industry the reviews of the period did justice, and a second edition of her book came out in 1845.

In 1874, Professor Jeb Mayor, of St. John's, Cambridge, at the request of his own and of Christ's Colleges, edited from materials left by the late learned antiquary, Charles Henry Cooper, a memoir of their foundress. This volume gives, in chronological sequence, every incident and detail which the most careful and minute research could make available for the Countess of Richmond's biography ; the Appendix has transcripts of her will and of many other documents, Latin and English, connected with her or with her foundations, while Professor Mayor, besides verifying the citations, correcting the clerical errors, and supplying Index and Glossary, has contributed some thirty pages of added or expanded matter.

Still, Cooper's "Memoir of the Lady Margaret," not being written in narrative form, appeals only to a very limited circle of readers : as Professor Mayor mentions that it was in the main written before 1840, "though the unwearied author added ever and anon new facts and references," it is probable that Mr. Cooper originally projected a complete biography, but on the appearance of Miss Halsted's volume deferred its completion. Now, however, that Miss Halsted's work has long been out of print, the occasion has surely arisen for a fresh narrative of one of those lives which, again to quote Cardinal Newman, "would instruct us in the capabilities of the English character, and make Englishmen love their country better, and on truer grounds." The present writer does not for a moment suppose that the following pages have done this adequately ; but if they become the occasion of a more competent hand's undertaking the task, the pleasant labour they have involved will not be a useless one.

THE KING'S MOTHER.

CHAPTER I.

MARGARET BEAUFORT, born at Bletshoe,

ERRATUM.

Page 45, footnote, *for* Leo XI. *read* Louis XI.

Somerset, and appointed Lieutenant-General
of the English possessions in France, which
post he held till 1436.

In 1444 Somerset, on some accusation
not specified, "of having been in league
with the King's enemies," fell into disgrace
at Court, and died within the year, at the

I

THE KING'S MOTHER.

CHAPTER I.

MARGARET BEAUFORT, born at Bletshoe, near Higham Ferrers, in Bedfordshire, in the year 1441, was the only child of John, first Duke of Somerset, by his wife Margaret, daughter and heiress of Sir John Beauchamp. Her father, who succeeded to the Earldom of Somerset on the death of his eldest brother, had won his spurs at Agincourt, and in the early years of Henry VI.'s reign he commanded the English forces in France. John Beaufort's best known exploit was the taking of Harfleur, in recognition of which he was made Duke of Somerset, and appointed Lieutenant-General of the English possessions in France, which post he held till 1436.

In 1444 Somerset, on some accusation not specified, "of having been in league with the King's enemies," fell into disgrace at Court, and died within the year, at the early age of forty-four — not without the suspicion of suicide. "The noble heart of so illustrious a man," writes the Monk of Croyland, "took the message of these unfortunate rumours so indignantly, that not being able to bear the strain of so great a disgrace, by his own procuring he hastened his death." This statement has been accepted without question by Sharon-Turner, Lingard, and other historians; yet it is worth noting that the Croyland chronicler was a strong Yorkist partisan, and is the only contemporary writer who hints that the Duke had other than a natural death. He was honourably interred in the Minster at Wimborne, a town to which the Lancastrian House always showed considerable favour, probably from the circumstance that Kingston Lacey lay close by, a residence that had belonged to John of Gaunt, and from him descended to the Somersets. The Duke's altar-tomb, ornamented with well sculptured alabaster figures, is still to be seen, though much defaced and broken. Of the estates left by the Duke of Somerset, a portion had been held by him as tenant for life, and passed with the ducal title to his brother Edmund; but the remainder was inherited by his only child and daughter, Margaret, who, within

three days of her father's death, was placed
under the wardship of William de la Pole,
Duke of Suffolk, though allowed to remaiı
under her mother's roof and care.

Three years later died the greatest of the
Beauforts, Henry, the Cardinal, In his boyhood he had been a student at Oxford, and
afterwards at Aix-la-Chapelle ; when only
eighteen he was made Bishop of Ely, and
later promoted to Winchester. In 1417, pro-
jecting an expedition to the Holy Land,*
he crossed to the Low Countries with a considerable retinue, rode up the valley of the
Rhine and so came to Constance, where a
Council of the Church was sitting. The
Papal See was vacant, and the Council
divided as to whether certain reforms ur-
gently needed in the Church should be
undertaken at once, or postponed till a new
Pope had been elected. The case was referred to the Bishop of Winchester, who
decided 'hat it was expedient first to elect a
Pope. His arbitration was accepted, and the
choice of the Council fell on Martin V.

At once a great Churchman and an en-

* Dean Milman, in his " History of Latin Christianity,"
alludes to Beaufort as having just then returned from the
Holy Land. But this is in direct contradiction to the very
detailed account in L'Enfans' " Histoire du Concile de Constance," followed by Hook in his " Life of Archbishop
Chicheley."

thusiastic Englishman, Beaufort's influence in public matters was considerable. In his earlier years he had, perhaps, too warlike a spirit for an ecclesiastic ; though he is not supposed to have advised the war with France, yet once it was begun he supported it strenuously. After Agincourt he made a historic speech in favour of following up the war, and it was the loan he then advanced which enabled Henry V. to march on Paris. But later in life Cardinal Beaufort evidently came to see that the French nation would never consent to be ruled by an English king, and that the effort to do so was ruining England; for he steadily pursued a peace policy, and by it drew intense unpopularity, both on himself and on his nephew, the Duke of Somerset. As to the merits of the incessant strife between him and the Duke of Gloucester, it is impossible now to form a positive opinion ; " but it is beyond all doubt, in the minds of all who have studied the subject, that Beaufort was not concerned in the death of Gloucester ";* and Lingard

* That Cardinal Beaufort's death was recognised as a national loss, is shown by a verse in the ballads of the time :

The Castle is won where care begun (Rouen),
    The Portcullis is laid down (Somerset),
Y-closed we have our velvet hat (Cardinal Beaufort),
    That sheltered us in many stormes brown.
        Wright's " Political Poems," Rolls' Series.

4

disbelieves Baker's account of the Cardinal's last moments, of which Shakespeare made so dramatic a use. To posterity Beaufort is best known by the munificence of his religious and charitable benefactions. By far the greater number were swept away at the Reformation, but on many an old building the portcullis of the Beauforts is plainly visible. In Winchester Cathedral it bears witness to the magnificent scale on which he completed William of Wykeham's work; and out of the innumerable similar foundations which once studded England, the Hospital of St. Cross,* richly endowed by him, is now the only one remaining where the bedesmen, still clothed in their ancient black gowns, and wearing the croix-paten on their breasts, still dwelling in the quaint but comfortable abodes Cardinal Beaufort built for them, keep up the mediæval tradition of hospitality and prayer.

Cardinal Beaufort's will, reprinted in Nichols' Collection, only mentions his charitable bequests, which were very large. His landed estates were for the most part inherited by his nephew, Edmund, second Duke of Somerset; while to Margaret Beaufort, who was his great niece, devolved the

---

* Situated one mile from Winchester.

5

manors of Amesbury and Wyterbourne, in Wilts, with Henxstrigge and Charlton Canvile in Somersetshire.

The Duchess of Somerset's first husband had been Sir Oliver St. John (from them are descended the Barons St. John of Bletsoe) ; about two years after the Duke's death she remarried with Lionel, Lord Welles, by whom she had one son, Leo ; both before and after her third marriage she continued to reside at Bletshoe, which was hers by inheritance. A portion of the site of the old castle of the Beauchamps is now covered by a farmhouse, but some traces of the mansion in which Margaret Beaufort's quiet and studious childhood was passed still remain.

In the middle of the fifteenth century the state of education was fairly good : no grown up persons above the labouring class seem to have been wholly illiterate ; "pennes, inke, and bokes" are frequently recurring items in the household accounts of well-to-do people ; and we see by the letters of the Paston family (which became connected by marriage with the Beauforts), that not only they, their friends, and their neighbours corresponded fully and fluently, but that even their domestic servants could write clear, well-expressed letters when the occasion required.* Girls of the lower and

* Preface to " Paston Letters," Ed. Gairdner.

middle classes, and the daughters of the smaller gentry, were mostly educated at the "she schools," of which Fuller, writing a century later, quaintly laments the loss— kept by inmates of the religious houses spread so widely over the country, who taught their pupils reading, needlework, French, and the rudiments of Latin. But children of a higher social class were less well provided for, as in order to prevent the spread of Wickliffe's tenets, a law had lately been passed, making it penal to have private tutors, so that boys and girls brought up at home, as was usually the case with the nobility, had not the same advantages as public school scholars ; probably the tutor of the Duchess of Somerset's children was either her domestic chaplain or the vicar of the parish. However, the Lady Margaret was taught French thoroughly, for she could converse freely and translate it easily. Of Latin she had only "a little perceiving, chiefly in the rubrics and the ordinal, and for the saying of the service which she well understood ";* in after life she regretted that she had not given herself seriously to study the language, "as she might easily have done." On the whole she seems, if not

* Fisher, " Mornynge Remembrance."

learned, to have been, at least, fairly studious; the retentive memory and ready wit that Erasmus admired when she was a very old lady, could not at any time have suffered from want of use. In needlework, she was considered to be very skilful, and there is yet preserved at Bletshoe a carpet worked by her with all the "arms and matches of the family of St. John;" probably the same which James I., when he hunted in the neighbourhood, asked to see, hearing it had been worked by his great grandmother."*

In very tender years the Lady Margaret had to exercise her judgment on a matter which does not trouble girls of our time, precocious as we think them, till a much later period. Henry VI. wished to secure her hand in marriage for his half-brother, Edmund Tudor; while her guardian, the Duke of Suffolk, pressed the suit of his own son, John de la Pole. To the latter some writers assume she was actually married by contract, on the ground that in the roll presented by Parliament to the King, impeaching the Duke of Suffolk, he is accused of "having proposed to marry to his son Margaret, daughter and heir of the late

* "Camden," by Gough. Vol. II., p. 5, Ed. 1806.

Duke of Somerset, and of having actually
caused her, since his arrest, to be so married." Against this may be quoted an incident Bishop Fisher relates in his "Mornynge
Remembrance" of the Lady Margaret, pre-
mising that he had often heard her tell it
herself:

"Being not yet fully nine years old, and
doubtful in her mind what she were best to
do (as to the marriage proposals made to
her), she asked counsel of an old gentle-
woman whom she much loved and trusted,
who did advise her to commend herself to
St. Nicolas, the patron and helper of all
true maidens, and to beseech him to put in
her mind what she were best to do. This
counsel she followed, but specially that night
when she should the morrow after make
her determination. A marvellous thing! The
same night, as I have heard her tell many
a time, as she lay in prayer, calling on St.
Nicolas, whether sleeping or waking she
could not assure, but about four o'clock in
the morning one appeared to her arrayed
like a bishop, and naming unto her Edmund
Tudor, bade her take him as her husband.
This she related to her parents (the
Duchess of Somerset had re-married with
Lord Welles), who willingly followed the

9

supernatural direction.". One wishes that some English Carpaccio had represented for us this little mediæval Ursula, lying in her curtained cot, "whether sleeping or waking she knew not," neither surprised nor disturbed, but meekly and gravely obedient to the heavenly vision.

Edmund Tudor, Earl of Richmond, to whom Margaret Beaufort was in her ninth year solemnly betrothed (their marriage did not take place till some years later), was son of Owen Tudor and of Katherine of Valois, the daughter of Charles VI., King of France, and widow of Henry V. of England. Queen Katherine's marriage had given great displeasure to the King's uncles, and when, eight years later, she died, her husband was imprisoned, and the custody of their children given to Katherine de la Pole, Abbess of Barking. But when Henry VI. assumed Royal authority, he at once released his step-father, and made his half-brothers, Jasper and Edmund Tudor, Earls of Pembroke and of Richmond, with precedence over all other Earls on account of their nearness to his person. And though Owen Tudor had but a moderate fortune, and was accounted no equal match for the Queen Dowager of France and England, he could

claim a longer lineage than either Valois or
Plantagenet, for he was descended from
Llewellyn, the last reigning Prince of Wales,
whose ancestry was traced upwards, through
Cadwallader to Uther Pendragon. So that
by the marriage of Edmund Tudor with
Margaret Beaufort came the first strain of
Celtic blood in the ancestry of our Royal
House, bringing with it something of the
Celtic mysticism—the glamour of an old
prophecy, spoken by Taliesin, the bard:
that one day the banner of the great Pen-
dragonship, carried by a descendant of Cadwallader, should bear down the standard of
the Leopard—a prophecy afterwards held to
be fulfilled on Bosworth Field.

But Margaret Beaufort's union with Edmund Tudor was of short duration; before
the year was out the little bride of fourteen
was left a widow, and the young Earl of
Richmond was buried in the house of the
Grey Friars at Caermarthen, whence, at the
dissolution of the monastery, his remains
were removed to the Cathedral church of
St. David, where, in the middle of the choir,
his altar-tomb of dark grey serpentine marble
still stands with half defaced escutcheons and
with an inscription, evidently written after
the accession of Henry VII.:

"Under the marble stone here inclosed resteth the bones of that most noble lord Edmond, Earl of Richmond, father and brother to Kings, the which departed out of the world in the year of our Lord God MCCCLVI. the third of the month of November : on whose soul, Almighty Jesus, have mercy."

Heu, Regum Genitor, et Frater, spendidus Heros,
    Omnis quo micuit regia, virtus obit,
    Herculeus comes ille tuus, Richmondia, duxque
    Conditur Edmundus his quoque marmoribus :
Qui regni clypeus, comitum flos, malleus hostis,
    Vitae dexteritas, pacis amator erat.
Hic meditare vians te semper vivere posse?
    Non morieris, homo? Nonne miselle, vides,
Caesar, quem tremeret armis nec vinceret Hector.
    Ipsa devictum morte ruisse virum?
Cede metrum precibus, det regnum conditor almus
    Ejus spiritui lucida regna poli.

And on the 26th January following, or the Feast of St. Agnes, 1456, the girl widow gave birth to a son, afterwards Henry VII., in a chamber which Leland's "Itinerary" tells us was still shown in the Castle of Pembroke in his time. It is probable that Henry VI. stood godfather to his little nephew, to whom his father's estates, excepting the portion settled on his mother for her dowry, were secured. In her vast possessions there were

mansions which would have made a brighter
and less secluded residence for the young
Countess than the gloomy Keep of Pembroke ; it was noted, as a proof of her prudence and discernment, that she chose to
bring her son up among his own kindred,
far away from the troubled currents of public
life.

Pembroke Castle had been in the preceding generation the residence of Gilbert
de Clare, Earl of Pembroke (better known
as Strongbow), before he married the
daughter of the King of Leinster, and
settled in Ireland. De Clare had strengthened the defences, built the stately Keep
which makes it even now one of the most
imposing castles in Great Britain, and
enlarged the domestic portions sufficiently
to render it a suitable home for a great
noble, at a time when security was held
to be cheaply purchased at the cost of
a certain amount of gloom and aloofness.
ˋ However, even with the protection of a
fortress castle, and despite the observances
with which custom in those days fenced round
persons of exalted rank, the position of a
widow was a difficult and perilous one for
the experience of barely sixteen years ; and
Lady Margaret was held by her contem-

poraries to have shown no inconstancy of affection, but rather a wise discretion when, after two years, she consented to marry her cousin, Lord Henry Stafford, a younger son of the Duke of Buckingham. But though the Lady Margaret proved an excellent wife, and was much beloved by her second husband's family, her strongest affections seem always to have been centred on her son and only child ; for, in the quaint phrase of an old chronicler, "though she was married to the Lord Henry Stafford, and again to the Earl of Derby, yet she never brought forth a child after, as though she had done her part when she had born a man-child, and the same a kynge of the realms." Henry VII.'s earliest biographer, Bernard Andreas, tells of Margaret's devoted care lavished on the boy who in his infancy was puny and somewhat delicate, so that his health was an anxiety to his mother, "who used to carry him about to many places in Wales, that he might thereby gain strength and agility."

That Henry himself had a vivid remembrance of his mother's care and love is proved by a letter written by him towards the end of his life, when, after acceding to a request she had made him, he goes on to say :

"And not only in this, but in all things

that I may know should be to your honour and pleasure and weal of soul, I shall be as glad to please you as heart can desire it ; and I know well that I am as much bounden to do it as any creature living, for the great and singular motherly love and affection it hath pleased you at all times to have for me."

We may think that there is nothing specially characteristic or singular in a mother showing tenderness to her only child ; but we have the testimony of a very careful and credible witness, the secretary of the Venetian Ambassador (writing a confidential report to his own Government *), that the English of those days were so cold and reserved towards their children as even to appear wanting in natural affection. The account which Lady Jane Grey gives of the sorrows of her childhood, the strict disciplinary rules framed by William of Wykeham and by Colet for their scholars, and some passages in the " Paston Letters " may be thought to give colour to this unfriendly criticism ; while on the other side we have a delightful picture by Erasmus of the household of Sir Thomas More. Again, though the outward manifestation of family

* " Italian Relation, 1500." Camden Society Edition, p. 21.

15

affection is not a thing to be despised, education in mediæval times, if it was to serve as a preparation for the future occasions of life, needed to be stern and strenuous; and just as in our day it is only the children of quite well-to-do people who reap the benefit of Solomon's theory of the rod, so in ancestral times it was in the higher ranks of society that the discipline of youth was most severe. Cardan, a distinguished mediæval physician, descanting on the great advantage of moderation carried even to austerity in food and drink, says: "This may easily be seen in the children of the nobility, so well brought up, merely on account of their spare diet, for it is not by stripes they are restrained." And Diego Taxades uses the growth of coral as an emblem of high bred youth: "Sprung from the midst of the waves, it is hardened by suffering, impervious to weather, and fit for the most precious purposes." * His mother's training, aided perhaps by the keen bracing air of the Welsh Highlands, did give to Henry of Richmond's temperament something of the hardness of coral: from having been a puny, delicate infant, he grew up strong, healthful, and vigorous in mind and body.

* Digby's "Mores Catholici."

From the scant records that have been gleaned, the years following the Countess of Richmond's second marriage seem to have been spent chiefly at Pembroke Castle. Notwithstanding their near kinship to the reigning House, and to the leaders of the two factions of York and Somerset that then divided the State (Lord Henry Stafford being nephew to Duchess Cicely of York, while Edmund, Duke of Somerset, Henry VI.'s favourite minister, was the Lady Margaret's uncle), she and her husband never seem to have frequented the Court. However, in this there was nothing singular; for just as in later days it was made a reproach to the upper classes that "They resort to the capital," in mediæval days the cry was "They flye to the country, few inhabit cities and towns, none have any regard for them." The literature, the traditions, the historic relics of the period show how much country was preferred to town by the gentry and nobility : how well those early makers of England knew where lay the hidden sources of her strength.

From her mother, a woman of great piety and zeal for religion, the Countess of Richmond had learnt to give the first hours of the day to religious exercises, and to fulfil

17

all her duties with promptness, diligence, and care.

"Her own household with marvellous diligence and wisdom this noble Princess ordered, providing reasonable statutes and ordinances, which she commanded to be read three or four times a year ; and oftentimes she would lovingly encourage them to do well, sometimes herself, sometimes by other persons. If there were any strife or controversy, she would with a great discretion study the reformation thereof.

"And what pains, O marvellous God ! would she take with the strangers : what labour she, of her very gentleness, would take to bear them company and entertain them, according to their degree and favour, and provide that nothing should lack that might be convenient for them, whereof she had wonderful ready remembrance and perfect knowledge."*

Hospitality, it must be remembered, is a word that carried in mediæval days a fuller meaning than it has with us who are inclined to regard it as a proof of kindliness, sociability, open-handedness—hardly as a serious virtue ; we ask to our houses those who please us, those who amuse us, those, perhaps,

* Fisher, "Mornynge Remembrance."

18

who we think will ask us again, and we have
our reward. But in those old world days, to
be hospitable meant to offer willingly good
entertainment to the weary wayfarer and the
belated traveller ; to have ever a kindly welcome for many of whom little or nothing save
their necessity was known ; to give refuge
and shelter to those whom the adverse
chances of war or some cruel injustice had
driven from their homes and possessions.
And even when the guests were friends or
kinsfolk, and the occasion joyful, there was
yet, as the good Bishop goes on to say (evidently from personal experience), " much
business in keeping hospitality ; the household servants must be kept in some good
order ; the strangers considered, those who
need it relieved and comforted."

Altogether, the ordering of a great mediæval household was no trifling matter ; constant
attention to details, as well as the " setting
forth of reasonable laws and ordinances,"
must have been needed. Much had to be
provided with forethought, not only for daily
use, but for possible emergencies; and though
trained and efficient servants were already to
be found, and were far better paid than
" clerks and scribes," of whom the multi-
plication of grammar schools and the dearth

of commercial outlets had brought about a plethora, yet owing to the backward state of civilisation the humbler workers in remote country places were sadly unskilled; while a glance through mediæval cooking-books and bills of fare shows that the domestic customs of our forefathers were by no means as simple as we might fancy. Great hunks of meat, even animals roasted whole, might be served to the household and retainers; but for the meals of the family and for festive occasions they had an immense variety of " made dishes." Even in the details of carving they were very precise; some thirty words, indicating important differences in the mode of dividing and distributing joints of meat, fowl, and game, have quite disappeared from our parlance. The arrangement and decoration of the table was also a care to the house-mistress : table linen was various in kind and quality, such as crass cloth, canvassers, diapers, naperies of Holland, Deventer, and Paris, all kept in quaint and beautiful chests, packed in rose leaves and sweet scented herbs. At the chief meals the table was "laid with a fair and clean cloth, and a napkin to each guest"; before sweets the board was cleared and fresh cloths and napkins, "couched fairly and honestly on the table, all to be done with great deliberation and adjustment"; and after dessert fingers were washed in silver ewers with scented water, and dried with napkins of very fine quality. Finally, when all in the house, gentle and simple, had been fed, came the turn of the poor, a certain number of whom would come daily to the gate of the castle or manor-house to receive the fragments that remained. And not only was the feeding and clothing of the poor part of a house-mistress' duties ; there was also the nursing of the sick —and an efficient training in this respect formed no small part of female education : for the question of allowing women to practice as doctors, or even as surgeons, was not then an open one ; that they should be prepared to do so was taken as a matter of course. In the pretty little thirteenth century tale of "Aucassin and Nicolette," it is told how when the former had fallen from his horse, the damsel Nicolette, after some skilful manipulation, found that his shoulder was dislocated, "whereupon she handled it with her white hands, and laboured so much that, by God's help, it came into place." There is no instance actually given of the Lady Margaret having shown such practical dexterity; but her knowledge of medicine is specially extolled, as well as the charity and kindness with which she habitually set apart a considerable portion of her time to prescribing for the poor and dressing their wounds. In later years it became her practice to arrange in her own mansions a sort of "hospital wing," in which twelve poor men and as many women were accommodated and attended to under her directions.

But the best part of the lives of the ladies and damsels of those old world days was spent in the open air. In castles built for defence the gardens were naturally restricted in space; still there would have been no lack of flowers in those small, carefully laid out enclosures : roses, red and white ; clove pinks, irises, purple and yellow ; scabious, holly-hocks, gilly flowers, peonies and columbines, with lilies of many kinds abounded ; while the snapdragon and valerian, which still grow in such profusion on the walls and turrets of old Welsh castles, suggest that no place was left idle where a seed could take root. And for the daughters of the House of Beaufort a castle garden should have had a special charm; for in all English verse there is hardly a more delightful picture of one than in the well-known passage of the "King's Quhair," where James I. of Scotland tells how he, a sad and weary prisoner in Windsor Keep, leant out of his window one fair May

morning, in the sweet hours of dawn, listening
to the lay of the nightingale, as she sang of
joy and love, and of the glory of the coming
summer. Then as the young King looked
down in the garden below him, full of birds
and flowers, he saw—

> The fairest and the freshest young flower
> That ever I saw, methought you that hour.

—the Lady Joan Beaufort, coming, like the
maidens in the miniatures, to gather flowers
in the dew at the foot of the gloomy prison
walls. To the Countess of Richmond, who
was Joan Beaufort's niece, that Royal romance,
with its poetic opening, its brief period of
married happiness, and its tragic end, must
have been very familiar ; and it is no unrea-
sonable stretch of fancy to think that she in
many ways moulded her own character and
life according to the model of her heroic aunt,
and that, when the duties, labours, and pleasures of the day were ended, the evenings
at Pembroke Keep would have been spent
much in the fashion described by the
Scottish chronicler of the Palace at Perth :
" in reading of romances, and singing, and
harping, and piping ; in playing of games,
and many other pastimes of great solace and
disport."

And just as the clangour of swords and

pikes, and the tread of armed men broke up the happy harmony of the Royal household at Perth, so did Pembroke Castle become the prey of invaders, who ruthlessly expelled Lord Henry Stafford and his wife from what they had thought would be their lifelong home; while to this trouble was added a far greater one—that her boy was taken from her before he had reached his sixth year, not from any fault of hers, but because both their lives were mixed in a web of history, so tangled, that to unravel it, the thread must be taken up many years back.

CHAPTER II.

IT is generally assumed that after the deposition of Richard II., his successor should have been Edmund, Earl of Mortimer, whose mother, Philippa, had been the only child and heiress of Lionel, Duke of Clarence, the third son of Edward III.

But Mortimer was a boy of only nine years, and besides neither law nor custom could then be quoted as absolutely determining whether the crown of England should, as by analogy to most landed estates, follow the female line, or be, as was usual with the honours of the Peerage, limited to heirs male. Nor could Continental kingdoms furnish a decisive precedent. In Germany the Emperors were elected, the great hereditary fiefs transmitted in the male line only ; the crown of Aragon went in the male, that of Castile in the female line also : and while in the kingdom of France the Salic law ruled the Royal descent, yet in the feudatory duchies daughters inherited when the direct male line failed ;

25

it was through an ancestress that the Kings of England claimed Aquitaine and Guienne. As far as popular English sentiment went, it is probable that if the Celtic remnant, as some writers tell us, formed the majority of the population, it would have been in favour of the inheritance going to the strong man of the family.

And "the strong man of the family," Henry of Lancaster certainly showed himself to be. After King Richard's deposition he summoned Parliament at once, and rising in his seat, challenged the crown: "As that I am descended from the good King, Henry III., and through that right God of His grace has sent me with help of my kin and of my friends to recover it, the which realm was on the point of being undone, through default of government and undoing of good laws."

Whereupon the two Archbishops, taking him by the hand, seated him on the throne, whence Henry once more addressed the assembly:

"Sirs," he said, to the prelates, lords, knights, and burgesses gathered round, "I thank God and you, spiritual and temporal, and all estates of the land, and do you to wit it is not my will that any man think that by way of conquest I would disinherit any of his heritage, purchase of other rights, nor put him out of the good things he has and has had by the good laws and customs of England, except those persons that have been against the good purpose and common profit of the realm."

Henry thus prudently avoided any precise definition of his claim, and neither he nor his son ever had reason to dread any questioning of the Lancastrian right. The only Plantagenet who could have put forward an adverse title was the Earl of Mortimer; but as he grew up to manhood a chivalrous and romantic friendship united him to the Prince of Wales, so that on succeeding to the throne, Henry V., far from fearing in his cousin a rival, could reckon on him as the most devoted of his friends and subjects, and on the accession of Henry VI., Mortimer was the first to tender his allegiance to the infant King. As he died childless, his immense possessions passed to the son of his deceased sister Philippa, Richard, Duke of York, who thus became the representative at once of Edward III.'s third son, Lionel, Duke of Clarence, and of his fifth son, Edmund Langley, Duke of York. In his childhood Richard was intimately associated with the House of Lancaster, his wardship having been assigned to Ralph Neville, Earl of Westmoreland, whose wife was Joan Beaufort, daughter of John of Gaunt (and consequently great-aunt to the Lady Margaret); he subsequently married their daughter. Nor did the reigning house show, in their treatment of the Duke of York, either jealousy or fear of any claim to the crown; on the departure of Henry VI. to France, York was appointed High Constable of England, and when the King's uncle, the Duke of Bedford, died, York was made Regent of France.

But as years rolled on, the troubles which had from the first beset the long reign of Henry VI. became more menacing; the King's pure life, gentle spirit, and unresisting meekness were only offences in the eyes of his turbulent subjects, and as one by one the great Lancastrian chiefs, Talbot, Bedford, and Gloucester, had passed away, the authority of the Crown grew weaker. The tragic end of Suffolk, the murders of the Bishops of Salisbury and Chichester, torn to pieces by the mob, were quickly followed by that sure sign of approaching anarchy— a temporarily successful insurrection. The common people, flattered by the perennial promise which then, at least, had the charm of novelty, " I will make it felony to drink small beer, and all the realm shall be in common," made to them by Cade, flocked to his camp at Blackheath, and for a time his power threatened to be formidable. However, his followers soon began to quarrel over their booty, the Londoners rose up and drove them into the Marshes, where the leader was easily captured.

Whether Cade's rebellion was actually fomented by Richard of York remains one of the problems of history; but it is commonly said that from that time forward the troubles of the reign were occasioned by the feud between the adherents of the Duke of York and those of the House of Lancaster. Still, the bitterness could not have been as great as is sometimes represented; for when, in 1455, a distressing malady fell on the King —he lost both reason and memory—and it became obvious that a regent must be named to act in his stead, the King's half-brothers, the Earls of Richmond and Pembroke, rode up to London in the Duke of York's company, evidently to support his claim to the post. Probably York's conduct was at that time conciliatory; but when he had been named by Parliament Protector of the Realm, he seemed at once to have adopted

regal style, and his first act was to send
Somerset* to the Tower. In the "Paston
Letters" is preserved an original letter
with York's title on the top, signed
with his own signet, bearing the arms of
England and France quarterly; while the
Duchess of York gave audiences in the
Throne Room of Fotheringay with a degree
of pomp and majesty Queen Margaret had
never assumed. After fourteen months, the
King's malady having left him as suddenly
and unaccountably as it came, York's Protectorate ceased and Somerset became once
more chief minister of the Crown. York
now took up arms and gained the victory
of St. Albans, where Somerset was slain
and the King made prisoner.

Apparently satisfied with this result, the
Yorkists treated Henry with the greatest
respect, asked his pardon, and renewed their
oath of allegiance. Three years later, in
1458, the pious Monarch endeavoured to
put an end to the incessant strife and con-
tentions that were ruining the kingdom by
a thorough and public reconciliation. A
solemn procession was made to St. Paul's
Cathedral. King Henry went first, in his
robes of state; behind him walked the con-

* Edmund, second Duke of Somerset; uncle to the
Countess of Richmond.

tending nobles, hand in hand : the young Duke of Somerset with Salisbury, Exeter with Warwick ; while the Duke of York, with great .show of familiarity, led the Queen. The ballads of the time tell of the joy with which the tidings of peace-making were received by the people ; but the truce was hollow and of short duration.

Then came the battle of Bloreheath, in which the Yorkists were victorious ; the Royal forces, however, rallied, and came on their adversaries at Ludlow. To silence the scruples of loyalty that were making some to waver, York had recourse to a dangerous stratagem ; he caused the rumour to be spread that Henry had died suddenly, and or-dered Masses for the Dead to be offered up. This was too much even for the meek-spirited King, who was roused to energy such as he had never shown before. He exhorted his troops " so knightly, so manfully, so comfortwise : with so princely a port and assured manner, that the lords and people took great joy; and only desired to fulfil his courageous desire." The Royal troops at-tacked and defeated the rebels before sun-set ; York fled in the night to Ireland, leaving behind him his wife and their four young children, who were committed to the

care of the Duchess' sister, the wife of the
Duke of Buckingham ; but a few months
later the tide of fortune completely turned.
Warwick rallied the disbanded Yorkist
forces, won the battle of Northampton,
drove Queen Margaret and her son into
exile, and before the year was out brought
the King a prisoner to London.

Up to this time the strife had been rather
what might be termed a contest for
leadership between the contending factors,
but now came a new departure. When Parliament met in October, 1459, the Duke of
York entered Westminster Hall with much
state and the blare of many trumpets, and
walking straight up to the throne he laid
his hand on it and stood silent, "like a man
meditating to take possession of his rights."
Then withdrawing it again he turned to the
Lords and bowed, whereupon the Archbishop
of Canterbury advanced and asked him to
go and visit the King. "I know of no man
in this realm who ought not rather to visit
me," was York's haughty rejoinder. The
next day he, for the first time, publicly
stated his claim to the crown, delivering
it in writing to the Lord Chancellor. The
Lords ruled that no subject could enter into
any communication in this matter without

the King's consent; when it was submitted
to him Henry replied, with simplicity and
dignity : " My father was King, his father
was King, I have worn the crown for thirty
years ; you have all sworn fealty to me as
your Sovereign. How, then, can my right
be questioned ? " But with his accustomed
conscientiousness, he desired they should
inquire into the matter. After hearing the
King's Serjeant and Attorney on the Royal
side, and York on his own behalf, even the
Yorkist lords (the Lancastrians had not been
summoned) were not unanimous. Some held
that when the direct male line failed, and the
representatives of females laid claim, the
crown might be considered in abeyance,
and that out of the rival candidates the
country could choose a King ; others pointed
out that the Duke of York bore the arms,
not of Lionel, Duke of Clarence, through
whose daughter he claimed, but those of
Edmund Langley, Edward III.'s fifth son.
At last they agreed to settle the matter by a
compromise, and decided that Henry should
keep the crown for his life, and York succeed
him. To this arrangement Henry VI. is
said, on the authority of Hall and of Grafton,
to have tacitly agreed.

However, Margaret of Anjou was not a

33

D

woman to submit tamely to the spoliation of her son's inheritance; she returned to England and raised the Royal standard in the provinces. Round her gathered the barons of the North under Lord Clifford, those of the West under the Duke of Somerset. York, defeated at Wakefield, December, 1460, was hurried to the block, and his head (according to a tradition which, however, has been disputed) was impaled on the walls of the city whence he took his title. The victory of Wakefield was followed up by another at St. Albans, and the Queen, eager to release her husband, marched on London. But her troops, flushed with triumph, plundered as they went, robbing even the churches and monasteries: they committed, according to the Croyland chronicler, deeds of sacrilege not exceeded at the Reformation. Seeing that they were looking forward to the sacking of London, and that if they entered the city she would be unable to control them, Queen Margaret halted at Dunstable.

Hither came the Recorder of London, with the Duchesses of Bedford and Buckingham (the late Duke of York's sisters) and Lady Scales, imploring peace and pardon, and at their request Queen Margaret appointed some Lords to reconnoitre the city and

obtain supplies. The delay was fatal to her
cause, for the young Duke of York had recruited an army on the Welsh border, and
defeated the Lancastrians, under Owen Tudor,
at Mortimer's Cross. In London the Yorkists
always had a strong following, and when the
Chancellor called together the populace in the
fields beyond Clerkenwell, and explained to
them Edward of York's claim, they warmly
supported him.

Whereupon sundry of the Lords and
Commons, hastily assembling at Baynard's
Castle, confirmed the election. Edward at
first hesitated, saying he had sworn fealty to
King Henry for his life; but when it was
represented to him there was no safety for
himself or for his supporters save by taking
the crown, he yielded, and was on the next
day proclaimed by the title of Edward IV.
Before the month was over the hopes of
the Lancastrians were extinguished, it was
thought for ever, at Towton, the bloodiest
battle ever fought on English soil.

In the proscription that overtook the Lan-
castrian leaders and the forfeitures that fol-
lowed—so merciless that for eight years the
King had no need to apply for money to
Parliament—the friends and relatives of the
Lady Margaret suffered cruelly. Her father-

in-law, Owen Tudor, together with the Earls
of Devon and Wiltshire, were beheaded at
Hereford ; the Duke of Exeter, though he
had married King Edward's sister, was driven
penniless into exile, "in the Low Countries,
where he was seen begging his bread from
door to door ; and with him that so unfortunate lord, the Duke of Somerset, and others
sharing their misery." One of Edward IV.'s
promptest attainders was that of the young
Earl of Richmond. Though he was a boy of
only ten years, his estates were given to the
King's brother, George, Duke of Clarence ;
while the custody of his person was assigned
to Sir William Herbert, to whom all the
possessions of Jasper, Earl of Pembroke, and
Pembroke Castle itself, were granted.

It was, of course, from the circumstance
of his being the nephew and godson of
Henry VI., on his father's side, and allied
through his mother with the hated House of
Somerset, that caused Harry of Richmond,
despite his tender years, to be dealt with
so severely. The Lady Margaret was treated
more leniently ; her estates, though at first
sequestrated, were given back to her by a
special Act of Restitution (1 Ed. IV., 1461),
which included both her dower and the lands
which had descended to her as the heiress

of John, first Duke of Somerset. For, drastic as were the proscription and confiscations of the Wars of the Roses, their effects were sometimes (though not always) softened by the circumstance of members of the same family being on opposite sides, so that even the vanquished had friends at Court. In the case of Lord Henry Stafford, while his father had been a staunch Lancastrian, and died fighting on the King's side at Northampton, his mother, Anne Neville, Duchess of Buckingham, was by birth daughter of the Earl of Westmoreland, York's guardian, and sister of the beautiful Cicely, now his widow. This relationship accounts for his presence, and that of the Countess of Richmond, at the solemn obsequies which Edward IV. had celebrated when the bodies of the late Duke of York and of his young son, George, Earl of Rutland, were removed in great state from Pontefract, where they had been hurriedly interred, to the burial-place of their family at Fotheringay. The remains, richly wrapped in cloth of gold, were put into a chariot covered with black velvet; at the Duke's feet stood a white angel bearing a crown of gold, to signify that of right he was King; the chariot was drawn by seven horses trapped to the ground, and every

37

horse carried a man. The bishops and abbots went on two miles in front to prepare the churches for the reception of the Princes *in pontificalibus*. After so travelling seven days, accompanied by a number of the nobility, and escorted by the Duke of Gloucester, the funeral train arrived at Fotheringay, where the King and Queen, with her two daughters, both infants in arms, and attended by many gentlewomen, awaited them. At the Mass of *Requiem* the Countess of Richmond offered after the Queen and her daughters.

Very slight record remains of the Countess' life at this period. In 1464 she and her mother, the Duchess of Somerset, were admitted into fraternity at the Abbey of Croyland, near the manor of Deeping, which was then held by the Duchess in dower, and which at her death descended to her daughter; but a good deal of her time, at least in the years immediately following Edward IV.'s accession, seems still to have been spent at Pembroke Castle; for her deep love for her son made her seek to be on friendly and even affectionate terms with the family of the Herberts, who were now the possessors. It is certain that Harry of Richmond was kindly treated and honourably brought up by the Lady Herbert, as if he had been one of her own family of many sons and daughters ; while his mother seems to have been allowed to choose his tutor, Andreas Scott, an Oxford priest, who afterwards spoke of young Richmond as "the quickest and most capable scholar he ever had." Still, kind as were his guardians, the lad was carefully watched, and never could forget he was a captive : for after he had grown to manhood we hear of his telling Philippe de Comines, that from the age of five he had been a prisoner—the one glimpse of liberty allowed him having been of such short duration as scarcely to count.

Such a victory as that of Towton might have been expected to end for ever the struggle of the rival Roses ; but by the indomitable energy of Margaret of Anjou it was prolonged for ten years. At one time rallying her English partisans, and risking battle ; at another seeking alliance abroad ; in perils by sea and land, now shipwrecked, now in the hands of robbers, the story of her adventures is a familiar page in the romance of history. When the fortunes of the Lancastrian House were at their gloomiest, the revolt of Warwick and Clarence lit them up with a flickering gleam.

It was with real reluctance that Queen Margaret had been brought to consent to an alliance between her son and Anne Neville, the daughter of their bitterest enemy ; its immediate result was that a fortnight later the news flashed through England that Warwick had landed at Ravensburg, and published a proclamation announcing that Queen Margaret and her son authorised him, together with Clarence, Oxford, and Pembroke, to raise the Royal standard. Within eleven days Edward had fled to Flanders, leaving his wife and daughters in sanctuary at Westminster, while Warwick had entered London and released King Henry.

It suggests a kindly nature in the eager partisan and dauntless soldier, Jasper, Earl of Pembroke, that at a time of intense excitement he made it his first business, on returning to England, to visit his sister-in-law at Pembroke Castle, where, at the suspicion of a Lancastrian reaction, she had been placed under the surveillance of the now widowed Lady Herbert. Jasper brought his nephew, then a boy of fourteen, back with him to London, and, according to tradition, took him to Eton. Though there is no written record of Harry of Richmond's stay at Eton, nothing is more likely than that Lord Pembroke should wish him to be educated at the great Lancastrian foundation, which his uncle and godfather, Henry VI., in earlier and happier days, had made in commemoration of the commencement of his personal reign. The gentle and studious King had spared no trouble in carrying out his design ; his mind, though never vigorous, was at that period clear, thoughtful, and conscientious. And to make himself thoroughly acquainted with the working of Wykeham's College, lately founded, and then considered the best school in England, Henry had spent many weeks at Winchester, studying the statutes, and making, in his own handwriting, alterations which secured to Eton boys as much liberty as was in those days thought compatible with necessary discipline. From the terraces of his Palace at Windsor he used to watch the progress of the buildings. By husbanding his resources, he was able to grant an endowment sufficient to give a free education to seventy carefully selected poor scholars ; while the statutes provided that twenty others of noble birth should be received, who, beyond their lodging, were to be no expense to the College. It was this last provision, unprecedented at the time, which has given to Eton its special character.

Cardinal Beaufort (Richmond's great-uncle) enriched the foundation by large legacies, besides a special bequest of the famous, almost priceless jewelled reliquary known as the " Tablet of Bourbon."

Among the Etonians of the period were the Paston boys, connected by marriage with the Beauforts; and the College records mention a present of fish and mushrooms offered to the Duke of Somerset, the kinsman of both Richmond and of the Pastons, who seems to have visited Eton just at this time, probably in the suite of Henry VI., who, on his release from eight wearisome years' captivity in the Tower, went to Windsor, and from thence paid a State visit to his favourite foundation.   It was then, so the legend runs, that being much struck by the "likely wit and towardness" of the handsome golden-haired lad, who was holding the ewer in which he was washing his hands, Henry VI. turned to the lords surrounding him, and said : " Lo ! surely this is he to whom we and our adversaries shall give place "—words which Shakespeare has paraphrased :

Come hither, England's hope : if secret powers
Suggest but truth to my divining thoughts,
This pretty lad will prove our country's bliss.
His looks are full of peaceful majesty,
His head by nature framed to wear a crown,

His hand to wear a sceptre ; and himself
Likely, in time, to bless a regal throne.
Make much of him, my lords ; for this is he
Must help you more than you are hurt by me.
Henry VI., Part III., Act iv., Scene 6.

Once more the Lancastrian triumph proved as transient as it had seemed complete : before six months had passed Edward IV. had landed at Ravenspur with a band of mercenaries, hastily recruited in the Low Countries ; and his great military talents (for he was accounted one of the best generals of his time) enabled him to regain possession of London—always Yorkist at heart—and to defeat the Lancastrians, first at Barnet and then at Tewkesbury. There he sullied his victory by much cruelty ; not only was Edward, Prince of Wales, a youth of seventeen, " slain fleeing townwards," but, after having promised to spare the lives of all who had taken refuge in Beaulieu sanctuary, when he found Somerset was among the number, the King broke his pledge, and on the day following the last of the male line of the Beauforts perished on the scaffold.

The Earl of Pembroke was hastening southwards with reinforcements, when news of the battle reached him. He immediately returned to Chepstow, where he spent some

43

time; put to death Robert Vaughan, who had been sent by King Edward with the design of entrapping him, and then retired with his sister-in-law and nephew to the Castle of Pembroke, where he was soon besieged by the victorious Yorkists. It was here that Harry of Richmond got his first experience of warfare : by the bravery of his uncle the enemy was kept at bay till a friendly reinforcement, commanded by David ap Thomas, came to their assistance. This chieftain, knowing that the lives of the Lancastrian leaders were at stake, had hastily collected a body of scantily armed but resolute Welshmen, and in the confusion that followed his attack on the besieging force, he conveyed the Countess of Richmond, with her son and Jasper Tudor, to Tenby, whence with a small attendance the latter set sail for France. One tradition runs that the Lady Margaret strongly opposed this course, and urged their trusting to the fortresses and fidelity of the Welsh; but Jasper, knowing how hopeless resistance was, persuaded her to acquiesce in their flight, and it has been said that she crossed the water with them, but was quickly compelled to return. That she did so is, however, unlikely, and is only suggested by a passage in Rymer, which to the present writer seems to bear a different meaning ; it is more probable that Lady Margaret parted from her son at Tenby. When safe out of England the trials of the fugitives were not ended : it had been Pembroke's intention to take his nephew to the Court of France,* where he had been most courteously received a few months before, when with the other English exiles he had rallied to the standard of Margaret of Anjou. But the elements were against the Lancastrians, a violent storm arose, and the wind being contrary, drove them on the coast of Brittany. They gained St. Malo with difficulty, and were resting themselves after their fatigues, when Duke Francis, having news of their arrival, sent orders that they should be arrested and conveyed as prisoners to his fortress of Vannes : a breach of hospitality which, though it cannot be excused, is accounted for by the importance which now attached to the person of Harry of Richmond, who since the deaths of Henry VI. and his son Edward, represented, in right of his mother, the English line of descent from John of Gaunt.

The founder of the House of Beaufort was John, first Earl of Somerset, the eldest

* The Dowager Queen Catherine, his mother, was aunt to the reigning Sovereign, Leo XI.

45

of four children borne previous to marriage
to John of Gaunt, Duke of Lancaster, by
Katherine—widow of Sir Otes Swynford—
who afterwards became his third Duchess.
Although this lady, the Bathsheba of our
Royal genealogy, is sometimes alluded to as
one of the most talented women of her time,
little is known of her save that she was a
daughter of Sir Payne de Roet, a Flemish
knight and King-of-Arms of the Province
of Guienne ; and that on the marriage of
John of Gaunt with his cousin, Princess
Blanche, she was attached to the person of
the young Duchess, her sister being *domi-
cella*, or, as it would now be termed, maid
of honour, to Queen Philippa.

Both sisters are said to have been extremely accomplished, and Katherine rose to
such favour with the Princess Blanche that
she gave her the charge of her children; and
though Katherine soon after married Sir
Otes Swynford, of Ketelthorpe, Lincolnshire,
she does not appear to have been wholly
separated from her Royal patrons, for it is
recorded that her husband was a knight in
the retinue of the Duke of Lancaster, and
that as such he received letters of protection
from him in Gascony (40 Ed. III., 1366). Sir
Otes Swynford died in 1370, and a year later

his widow became the acknowledged mistress
of the Duke of Lancaster. He ·gave her
the Castle and lordship of Beaufort, in
Anjou, and there were born their children—
John, afterwards created Earl of Somerset ;
Thomas, Duke of Exeter ; Joan, who became
the wife of Ralph Neville, Earl of Westmoreland, therefore grandmother to Edward
IV. and Richard III.; and Henry, Cardinal
Beaufort. It was from their birth in the
patrimonial castle of the Lancasters that the
Beauforts bore as their cognisance the portcullis, which is introduced into almost all the
finest architectural buildings in England that
have survived from the fifteenth century.

Soon after the death of his second wife,
Constantia of Castille, John of Gaunt married Lady Swynford, and in the year following he obtained the legitimation of his
children by her : first, in a Bull granted by
Pope Urban VI., then by a charter from his
nephew, Richard II., and finally by Act
of Parliament confirming those indulgences,
without any restriction with respect to their
claim to the throne.*

* " Excerpta Historica," p. 152. Leland, indeed, says that
John Beaufort, Earl of Somerset, was born after the marriage
of Katherine Swynford and John of Gaunt, but this can
hardly be reconciled with the patent of legitimation before
referred to. On the other hand, that he should have used
the name of Beaufort, rather than that of Plantagenet, is

After his marriage with her sister, John of Gaunt is said to have settled on the wife of Chaucer the Castle of Donnington, in Suffolk, as a testimony of goodwill and to mark their consanguinity. In 1397 he died; the Duchess Katherine survived him four years and then was buried in Lincoln Minster, where, on the west side of the altar, her monument still remains.

John Beaufort, the eldest son of Katherine Swynford, was created Earl of Somerset in the lifetime of his father, September 29th, 1397; his seals contain the entire arms of John of Gaunt, viz., France and England, quarterly, within a bordure, gobony, argent, and azure. Richard II., who had always been warmly attached to his uncle of Lancaster, continued after his death to treat the Beauforts with marked kindness and distinction, and they proved their gratitude by dissociating themselves from the rebellion of their half - brother, Henry, Duke of Lancaster. And in November, 1399, the Earl of Somerset, with his brother, the Earl of Dorset, and

not a proof of illegitimacy, for the use of surnames at that period was still very irregular. For instance, the fifth son of Edward III. bore the name of Edmund Langley, and we find that the eldest son of John Beaufort, John, Duke of Somerset (the father to the Lady Margaret), was styled the Lord John Plantagenet (Vitellius, chap. xvii., f. 328) (Cooper's " Memoir of Margaret Beaufort)."

other noblemen of inferior rank, partisans of
Richard II., were arrested and commanded to
forfeit all the lands they held. But shortly
after Henry IV. relented, made public proclamation of his confidence in his dear
brother, John, Earl of Somerset, restored
his possessions, and appointed him Lord
Chamberlain of England. In January, 1400,
the Earl of Somerset was given command
of four thousand men to put down the revolt
headed by the Earl of Huntingdon. Still,
Henry IV. must have retained some unfriendly feeling towards the Beauforts as in
1407 he caused to be inserted in their patent
of legitimation an interlineation excepting
them from the Royal dignity.

There is no evidence as to whether the
circumstance of the interlineation having
been made was known to the Earl of Somerset; in any case, as Henry IV. had two
brothers and three sons, it did not immediately affect his interests, and might have
been dangerous to dispute. And when time
passed on, and all the elder Lancastrian lines
had died out, Harry of Richmond had become heir-general of John of Gaunt, and
the uncontested representative of the House
of Lancaster; and when the question of the
descent of the Crown came to the front, all

49

those who could have remembered how the patent first ran had passed away ; thus it seems to have been accepted that the limitation was included in the original document. Indeed, most of the earlier English historians so describe it.*

* Of course, if a later insertion, the Clause of Limitation would be quite inoperative, even if inserted at the command of the reigning Sovereign; for it could not affect a previous Act of Parliament publicly assented to by King, Lords, and Commons.

"The legality of the Royal Act which barred the Beauforts from succession to the Crown was more than questionable ; they themselves never admitted it, and the conduct of Henry VII. points to a belief in their rights. Their male line was extinguished by the death of the last Duke of Somerset, at Tewkesbury, and the claim of the house was believed to rest in Margaret Beaufort" ("History of the English People" : J. R. Green).

Extract from the patent of legitimation granted by King Richard II., February, 1397, showing the interlineation supposed to have been made by order of Henry IV. in 1307 ("Excerpta Historica," p. 3) : "We do, in fulness of our Royal power, and by the assent of Parliament, by the tenour of these presents, empower you to be raised, promoted, elected, assume, and be admitted to all honours, dignities, *excepting the Royal dignity*, pre-eminences, estates, and offices, public and private, whatever, as well perpetual as temporal."

Witnessed by the King at Westminster the 9th day of February, 1397.

CHAPTER III.

THE young Earl of Richmond's claim to the English crown received considerable confirmation from the conduct of Edward IV., who on hearing of the escape of the Earl of Pembroke and his nephew became violently excited, and was only appeased on learning that they had not reached France, but were detained by his ally, the Duke of Brittany. He now offered to ransom them at any cost ; but by thus betraying his fears he heightened their value in the estimation of the wary Duke, who, while accepting the gifts proffered to him, yet declared he could not in honour surrender the persons of those whom the chance of fortune had laid under his pro-, tection. He pledged himself, however, for their safe custody, engaging to keep so strict a watch over their actions that the King of England could by no possibility be endangered, either in his person or his throne.

With this promise Edward had to be satisfied ; while the Duke, to carry it out to the letter, sent the Earl of Pembroke to a distant fortress. While young Richmond was kept a prisoner at Vannes, his personal attendants were dismissed, and native Bretons, chosen by Duke Francis, placed about him in their stead. This severe treatment, however, became as time passed on gradually somewhat relaxed ; the quiet submission with which he bore the privations and restrictions imposed on him created a feeling of compassion in those who were charged with his custody, and bespoke for him the kindly interest of Duke Francis' consort, Margaret, daughter of Gaston de Foix, a very noble and accomplished woman. Happily for Richmond, he was by nature gifted with a peculiar sweetness of manner and address. Philip de Comines, who knew him well, testifies that he was perfect in courtly breeding and handsome in person. From the first year of his exile he set himself to study the French language, and spoke it gracefully.

While, by his vindictive pursuit of young Harry of Richmond, Edward IV. betrayed that he feared in him a rival aspirant to the throne, the Lancastrians, on the other hand, showed by their demeanour after Tewkesbury that they considered themselves released from their allegiance to the Red Rose. The country was weary of civil war, and the very principle of loyalty prompted them to submit to King Edward, whose claim by right of birth was at least equal to any that could be opposed to him. To Queen Margaret no allegiance was due, and she who had shown such desperate tenacity in defence of her son's rights was now utterly crushed and broken-hearted ; even by her enemies she is admitted to have behaved with great dignity and propriety, encouraging those who had so long clung to her fortunes to make the best terms they could for themselves. Morton, the most faithful of all, sent in his submission, and the Countess of Richmond, with the discretion which always marked her actions, endeavoured, by leading a life of strict privacy in the most secluded portions of her estates, to avert Edward's anger from her husband and herself, and soften it towards her son.

For some time she seems to have resided at Torrington, in Devonshire. There is a record that, on finding the priest's house to be a long distance from the church, she bestowed on him and his successors a manorhouse and the lands appertaining to it, more conveniently situated. Her footsteps can also be traced by charitable foundations at

Hatfield and at Fordham, and it is probably at this time that she erected the altar-tomb in Wimborne Minster, which still marks the resting-place of her parents, the Duke and Duchess of Somerset, and founded there a chantry, with grammar school attached. But her principal residence was at Colyweston, in Northamptonshire, where she built a stately mansion, on the site of one begun by Lord Cromwell, the Lord High Treasurer to Henry VI. The property on which it stood was made valuable by large slate quarries, and her benevolence found scope in ministering to her poor neighbours and giving them employment. Charity, it has well been said, was the mainspring of Margaret Beaufort's every thought and action, leading her to shun the paths of discord and follow those of peace.

From the number of occupations and interests in which, after her son's accession, the Countess of Richmond's life was passed, we may be sure that at this earlier period it was full and vigorous. Ill-health she never seems to have known : her journeys, which were frequent, we ascertain incidentally to have been made on horseback ; and Blessed Fisher tells us that in her hours of leisure she used to " recreate her mind with reading

and translating from the French books profit-
able to religious meditation." The trans-
cribing of books, in those days when it was
only through that tedious process they could
be multiplied, was accounted a most meri-
torious work : still more useful was that of
translation, which, now that dictionaries are
common and books of reference easy of access is not very difficult, but in former times
implied some industry and talent. As regards purity of diction and choice of language, Lady Margaret's writings may be
regarded as standard specimens of the good
English of the age. Her translation of the
" Imitatio Christi " will be more fully referred
to in another chapter.

That her studious habits were known and
appreciated is shown by the bequest made to
her by her husband's mother, the Duchess of
Buckingham, who died in 1480. " To my
daughter of Richmond, a book of English
called ' Legenda Sanctorum,' a book in
French called ' Luccan,' another book in
French of the Epistles and Gospels, and a
Primer with clasps of silver gilt, covered
with purple velvet ; " a gift of no small value
at a time when books were worth more than
their weight in gold : from twenty to fifty
pounds being an ordinary price for a slender

volume, and the purchasing power of money about fifteen times greater than it now is.

About five years after the Countess of Richmond's separation from her son a very serious danger threatened him. The vigilance pledged by Duke Francis had by the time Harry of Richmond reached his twentieth year become gradually relaxed : he had occasional access to the Court, and was allowed to follow some of the pursuits natural to his age and rank. Handsome in person (as Philip de Comines testifies), " perfect in courtly bearing," with already the tact and readiness which afterwards astonished the Spanish Ambassador Ayala—for his adversities had ripened him quickly—he had gained many friends; so that a party seemed to be forming, both in Brittany and France, of persons of influence, who, if not disposed at once to favour his pretensions, at least wished ultimate success.

King Edward, a great master in diplomacy, now affected to be gratified by the accounts which reached him of his young kinsman, and to be concerned for his welfare. He despatched Stillingfleet, Bishop of Bath and Wells, as his envoy to Duke Francis, with the proposal that Richmond should marry his daughter, the Princess Elizabeth. The

subtle design succeeded, and Duke Francis
handed Richmond over to the persuasive
Bishop, with an armed escort to take them
to St. Malo, lest he should try to escape to
France. Providentially, contrary winds detained them, Henry fell ill of fever, and his
entreaties, combined with a representation
of the persecution he had suffered and the
danger of his return to England, so wrought
on the Admiral of Brittany, Jean de Quelenac,
that he connived at the captive's removal to
the sanctuary of St. Malo, whence the English envoys were powerless to withdraw him.
Time being thus gained, Quelenac and Landois, the Duke's Treasurer, succeeded in
proving to Francis that treachery was intended, and Stillingfleet had to return empty-
handed to his master, having only succeeded
in getting a compromise, by which Richmond
was once more consigned as a prisoner to
Vannes, and communication with his mother
became again difficult. Still, she never
ceased to correspond with him, and to
supply his needs.

In 1482 the Countess of Richmond became
for the second time a widow. It is certainly
somewhat strange that Lord Henry Stafford,
who in his own right was a person of
considerable importance, should never be

mentioned, except in relation to his marriage and death, in any chronicle or public record. Still, this hardly affords ground for the inference drawn by a writer in the *Dublin Review* (Vol. VIII., p. 144), that the Lady Margaret's marriage with him was one of policy rather than of affection, and that this "kinswoman of thirty kings never merged the princess in the wife;" and that in both her later marriages she "devoted herself to the well-being of her son, rather than in that of her lord"; while the eulogium passed on her by Miss Halsted, "that in the performance of her conjugal duties she is justly held up as a bright mirror to her sex," also goes beyond what is actually known. Still, for the last assumption there is this ground, that her husband's father and mother both mention her affectionately in their wills, and that Lord Henry named her his sole executrix, styling her "his entirely and best-beloved wife, Margaret, Countess of Richmond," and expressed much anxiety that all the lands and manors that were promised him by his father, the Duke of Buckingham, should be secured to her.

It would seem that at the time of his death Lord Henry Stafford and his wife were living at Woking, in Surrey, as his will is witnessed by Walter Baker, vicar of the parish; also that they had long sojourned there, for he bequeaths to the high altar of the same church "ten shillings for offerings, forgotten or withholden, and twenty shillings for works to the same sacred edifice; to his stepson, the Earl of Richmond, a trapper of four new horse harness of velvet." Other bequests of some interest are those of his bay courser to his brother John, Earl of Wiltshire; and of his grizzled horse to Reginald Bray, an old follower and trusty friend of the Stafford family, whom the Countess of Richmond continued in her service, making him steward of her household, and whom we shall subsequently find employed in important missions.

A few months later, at a date not precisely ascertained, the Countess suffered a fresh loss in the death of her mother, the Duchess of Somerset. She was interred by her husband's side in the tomb in Wimborne Minster, on which still are their effigies; but the inscriptions and escutcheons which once embellished it have disappeared.

Not a very long period had intervened when the Countess of Richmond entered for the third time into matrimony with her cousin Thomas, the second Lord Stanley, whose

59

first wife, by whom he had a numerous family, had been sister to the Earl of Warwick and to the Duchess of Buckingham (the mother of Lord Henry Stafford). So far back as the battle of Bloreheath Stanley had been a staunch supporter of the House of York, and now held the office of Steward of the King's household, standing high in the Royal regard. In the middle and lower ranks of society at that period even second marriages were regarded with disfavour ; but in troubled times they were practically a necessity for women with great possessions, unless they entered a religious order. It is probable the Lady Margaret would rather have chosen this alternative, and that she married Lord Stanley chiefly to secure for her son, in whom all her thought and affections were bound up, the help and protection of one of the most powerful families among the great houses in the realm. The immediate result of her marriage was to draw the Countess away from the secluded country life she seems always to have preferred, as Lord Stanley, being of the King's Council, had to reside chiefly in London, where he had lately built himself the princely mansion, known later as Derby House, on St. Benet Hill, near where the Heralds' College now stands. Her position as the nearest living representative of the House of Lancaster at the Court of Edward IV. could not have been an easy one; it seems to have been recognised that hers was but a negative allegiance, contrasted with the personal and zealous loyalty of her husband, if the words Shakespeare puts into the mouth of Edward IV.'s Queen may be taken as a fair illustration of the situation :

STANLEY : God make your Majesty joyful as you have
    been.
QUEEN ELIZABETH : The Countess Richmond, good my
    lord of Stanley,
    To your good prayer will scarcely cry, " Amen."
    Yet, Stanley, notwithstanding she's your wife
    And loves not me, be you, good lord, assured,
    I hate not you for her proud arrogance.
STANLEY : I do beseech you, either not believe,
    The envious slander of her false accusers,
    Or, if she be accused on true report,
    Bear with her weakness, which, I think, proceeds
    From wayward sickness, and no grounded malice.
               Richard III., Act i., Scene 3.

It needs, perhaps, the license of poetry to be justified in describing the English capital at the time when the Countess of Richmond took up her abode in Derby House as :

    A London, small and white and clean.

But it had many pleasant characteristics now irreparably lost. And the inhabitants were

proud of their city : " placed by Nature on a
little hill, round whose base the Thames
flowed like a bow bent, or crescent moon," as
bright when the sunlight dances on its waters
as Diana's emblem. Very specially proud
were they of London Bridge, " one of the
wonders of the world," with its nineteen great
arches of massive stone, " so furnished with
shops that passengers might take it for a
fair street," thronged with busy people mov-
ing to and fro ; clad in quaint, bright coloured
garments, various in texture and in cut, those
of the wealthier classes rich and somewhat
fantastic, for " the English have always been
remarked for their love of fine clothes,
superfluous and changeable." Beside their
extravagance in dress, our ancestors were
also distinguished from other Cisalpine na-
tions by their excellent manners, they were
" extremely polite in their language ; in
addition to their civil speeches, they have
incredible courtesy in remaining with their
heads uncovered with admirable grace while
they talk to one another."*

Probably time was of less value in the city
than now, yet the tokens of wealth were
striking. " In the Strand," says the same
writer, " there are fifty goldsmiths' shops

* " Italian Relation," p. 22 (" Calendar of State Papers ").

better than could be found in five Italian
cities, with wonderful quantities of wrought
silver, salts, cups, and ewers." In the less
important thoroughfares, women might be
frequently seen doing their shopping in a
comfortable, convenient fashion ; for the shops
opened mostly on a raised stone pavement,
with arcades for shelter, as we see them now
in the old streets of Chester, each trade represented by its sign affixed to the house or
hanging from the door. Taverns were not
unfrequent, but they were used for games
and athletic exercises rather than for exces-
sive drinking. As in all countries where
those wonderful builders, the Romans, had
not left their mark, the secular buildings were
neither high nor massive ; it was not until
the next century that the tall houses were
accused of depriving Londoners of the sight
of Heaven. And there were plenty of open
spaces, the air was sweetened with the per-
fumes of the roses and eglantines growing
over the walls of gardens, many of which
were of considerable size, especially that of
the Friars Preachers in the Farringdon
Ward ; and the great garden at Holborn
was later attached to the Palace of the
Bishops of Ely, where in the times of the
De Lacys wine and cider used to be made.

Bishop Morton, who was a skilled horti-
culturist, supplied the Londoners with early
vegetables, choice fruit, and the straw-
berries not to be surpassed, which, together
with the red and white roses of the Temple
Garden, have their niche in history. The
Londoners dearly loved flowers and everything that recalled country life : in the summer months, on the eve of any Church
festival, * every man's door would be
shadowed with green boughs, with branches
of fennel, St. John's wort, orpins, and white
lilies ; among them tiny lights were scattered, while those householders who could
afford it hung out branches of iron, which
was then beginning to be very curiously and
beautifully worked, each carrying, perhaps,
as many as fifty lamplets. In the open places
bonfires were burnt, so called as signs of
good amity ; for it was held that the festivals
could not be better celebrated than by the
reconciliation of all who had quarrelled or
were in enmity, the neighbours making it
a joy to bring them together. Moreover,
these fires of wood were thought to purify
and sweeten the air, so that to provide them
was a good work. It was also customary for

* Of these summer festivals the best known was the
Feast of St. John the Baptist's birth ; but these ways of
honouring them were common to all.

the rich to put out tables in front of their houses with plenty of good viands, of which they would invite their poorer neighbours to partake.

Doubtless there were blemishes in the picture, gloomy lanes and courts inhabited by the very poorest ; not banished as they now are to distant quarters, but mixing incongruously with the mansions of the great lords and of the rich citizens. Still, the Londoners had a good understanding of the need of sanitation, and keen olfactory nerves. The most unpleasant trades, as of butchers, dyers, leather workers, and the like, might not be carried on nearer than Knightsbridge or Stepney ; and when, in defiance of many contrary ordinances, persons unduly covetous of gain tried to introduce into their workshops the noisome sea coal, the honest citizens came out in their wrath, and with clear consciences threw the odious sacks into the Thames.

And even if sanitary ordinances were made only to be broken ; if the efficiency of watchmen and of the scavengers would not have satisfied the requirements of a modern vestry ; after every unsavoury detail, scattered through centuries of record, has been piled up into one big indictment of mediæval

London, there still remains the rebutting evidence of the merry, bright scaled fish leaping in the great fosse of the Tower; the tradition of a long procession of salmon coming up from the sea in the happy springtime, making their way rejoicing, despite of nets and of anglers, to spend the summer in the pools and reaches' of Berks and Oxon.

If, as we have seen intimated by Shakespeare, the relations between the Countess of Richmond and Edward IV.'s Queen were not cordial, she was probably on still more distant terms with his mother, the Duchess of York, who was then living at Baynard Castle, which, in the Lady Margaret's early married life, had been the town house of the Tudors. But in the Bishop of Ely, who was a still nearer neighbour at Holborn, she had an old and steadfast friend; for Morton, although high in favour with the King, never quite forgot his Lancastrian proclivities, and was the trustee of the Countess of Richmond's marriage settlement with Lord Derby. Their characters had much in common, as the Bishop, whose later fame rests chiefly on his statesmanship, was in those earlier days a distinguished patron of literature, and an active philanthropist interested

in all the social questions of the time. And,
as becomes a bishop, he was given to hospitality ; the bill of fare which has survived
from one of his great banquets is probably
the most complete and ample ever written
out in English. This, however, implies no
reflection on Morton's personal habits, which
were frugal and abstemious, as all may see
from . the well - known passage in More's
" Utopia," describing "that beautiful household, through which a soul more beautiful
shone." And round Morton gathered the
best workers and thinkers of the period, one
of the most interesting in history ; for it is
curious to note that " the marvellous interval
from 1450 to 1510, which saw the fall
of Constantinople, America discovered, the
East explored, the system of the heavens
.explained, in which printing, engraving,
paper, gunpowder started suddenly into
being," exactly coincides with the span of the
Countess of Richmond's life ; so that eager,
sympathetic spirit must, at every decade,
have been stimulated by fresh energies and
interests. In the earlier period of the Renascence, when the mediæval mind first began
to turn to the older fountains of knowledge,
and strive to recover the lapsed inheritance
of the past, Italy, from her unbroken con-

nection with the ancient world, naturally took the lead; but there was a moment when England seemed likely to hold a good second place. Among Universities, the reputation of Oxford stood very high; and no Cisalpine names were more honoured in Italy than those of Humphrey, Duke of Gloucester, to whom Aretino dedicated his translation of Aristotle and his Plato : and of that terribly Italianised Englishman, John Tiptoft, Earl of Worcester, of whom it is recorded that the elegance of his Latinity drew tears from the eyes of Pope Pius II. (Eneas Sylvius), himself a man of letters, alive to all the delicacies and ingenuities of humanistic rhetoric.

But the Wars of the Roses threw England back for two generations, and when they had ended the work had to begin again. However, as often happens on soil that has lain fallow, the seed grew up quickly. In 1472 Caxton set up his first printing press; twelve years later it was boasted that the English, who formerly were indebted to the Venetians for their books, now exported them to Italy. However, the period was one rather of quiet working than of brilliant initiative : Grocyn and Linacre were studying under Greek masters in

Italy ; Colet's name was as yet hardly known, and More was still in his boyhood. The most interesting figure seated at Morton's hospitable board must have been the brilliant, accomplished Lord Rivers, the Picus Mirandula of the English Renascence, who in the preface to his translation of the " Dictes : or, Notable Sayings of the Philosophers," which was the first book printed on English ground, tells so simply how the little volume was lent him as he was starting on a pilgrimage to Sant' Iago di Compostello, but, finding the subject not consistent with the dispositions that belong to a maker of pilgrimages, he refrained from opening it ; but on his return read it with delight, and forthwith translated it for his friend Caxton to publish.

It was not until a later period that the Countess of Richmond became a helpful and munificent patron of Caxton. At the period following her marriage with Lord Stanley she naturally took a less prominent position, especially as, for the most part, her husband was not with her at Derby House, but commanding a force sent to support the Duke of Gloucester, who was fighting on the Scotch frontier. While Richard pressed forward towards Edinburgh, Lord Stanley, with four thousand men, bésieged Berwick, and after a fierce struggle took it by assault.

There seems to have been some jealousy between Gloucester and Stanley, for an old MS. poem written by Robert Glover, Lancaster herald under Queen Elizabeth, has a quaint description of a quarrel in the course of which Stanley drove Gloucester over Salford Bridge and captured his standard :

> Jock of Wigan, he did take
> The Duke of Gloster's banner,
> And hung it up in Wigan Church,
> A monument to his honour.

However, the dispute does not appear to have had any serious result, as no more is heard of it during the remainder of the campaign, which was interrupted by the news of the King's sudden illness. Stanley hurried back to London in time to be present at the death of Edward IV., who made him one of the executors of his will, and guardian to his eldest daughter, the Princess Elisabeth—a trust Stanley kept faithfully and loyally, but at his utmost peril.

CHAPTER IV.

DURING the latter years of Edward IV.'s reign two parties had divided the kingdom. On the one side was that of the "Queen's friends," composed almost exclusively of her relations, among whom the most distinguished were her brother, Lord Rivers, and a few recently ennobled gentlemen. But though few in number, the "Queen's friends" filled many important official posts, and at the moment of King Edward's death the guardianship of the Prince of Wales—who by Elizabeth's orders, when his father expired, had been sent, under Lord Rivers' care, into Wales—was in their hands. Opposed to them were the old nobility, and the adherents of the House of York; of this party, the Duke of Gloucester was naturally the chief. His conduct at the time of his brother's decease was honourable and loyal: after a solemn funeral service celebrated at York, he summoned the Northern nobility to swear fealty to the young King, after which he wrote the Queen a kindly and brotherly letter. But when Richard found that Elizabeth was endeavouring to keep, not only the custody of her son's person, but the government of the realm, in her own hands, he promptly asserted his rights, met Rivers and Grey, with his nephew, on their way to London, transferred the young King to his own keeping, and had his claim to the Protectorate confirmed by the Privy Council. In all this Gloucester had the approval of every class in the nation, including those who were especially known to have been the late King's personal friends : Hastings, Stanley (whom Edward, as already stated, had at his death appointed guardian to his daughter Elizabeth), and Morton, Bishop of Ely. But though these men recognised the necessity of dealing firmly with the Queen Dowager, knowing that her policy would, if successful, lead to civil war, they were also anxious that the Duke of Gloucester should be merely President of the Council of Regency, not supreme head of the State ; through Elizabeth, who since her brother's imprisonment was driven to turn to them for help, they quickly obtained influence over the young King's mind, and imagined that, as soon as Edward was crowned, Gloucester's Protectorate would

cease and a new arrangement be made.
Richard, discerning their views, resolved
that his nephew never should be crowned,
and prepared what in modern parlance
would be called a *coup d'état*.

On Friday, the 13th of June, 1483, took
place the famous "strawberry scene" evolved
by Shakespeare from Morton's narrative to
More—of which the outcome was the
summary execution of Hastings and the
committal to the Tower of the Archbishop
of York, the Bishop of Ely, and Stanley—
the only one of the party who seems to
have suffered actual violence ; a soldier having struck violently at him with a pole-axe,
so that he fell, covered with blood. But
the blow, though severe, did not endanger
Stanley's life, and was probably only intended to keep him from taking any part
in the events of the next few days, during
which the progress of affairs was rapid. On
June 18th, five days after the "strawberry
scene," Bourchier, Archbishop of York, went
to the Queen, who had taken refuge in
Westminster Sanctuary, and on his pledging
himself for the boy's safety, persuaded her,
despite her pitiful resistance, to give up the
little Duke of York into his charge. During
the days which followed, doubts as to the

validity of Edward IV.'s marriage with Elizabeth Woodville were sedulously circulated:
on the 24th a deputation, headed by Buckingham, went in procession to Crosby Place, the
private dwelling-house of the Protector, and
personally solicited him to be their King. After
a well-acted scene of hesitation, Richard ac-
ceded to their request, and when Parliament met on the day following, a roll was
presented, claiming the crown for the Duke
of Gloucester, on the ground that the late
King's marriage was invalidated by a pre-
contract with Dame Elinor Butler; and that
the line of Clarence being attainted, Richard
was his father's heir. Whereupon, the Lords
and Commons, "with one universal negative
voice, refused the sons of King Edward, and
proclaimed the Duke of Gloucester King."

There is no question but that at this period
of his life Richard III. was extremely popular; the great body of the Yorkists were
zealously attached to him; the Lancastrians
willing to give him a fair trial; the sober
citizens of London pleased to have a Sovereign who would abstain from the violations
of decorum into which his high spirits had
often led King Edward; while with the
common people, Richard's great affability
and the splendour of his tastes made him

almost as great a favourite as his brother had been. Nor did he neglect any means of improving his position ; immediately on his proclamation he began to sit in the Courts of Law, saying, " It was the King's chief business to administer justice "; he let no man's salute pass unnoticed, and on July 4th went to the Tower and transferred the Bishop of Ely, whose imprisonment had displeased the Universities, to the milder custody of Buckingham, after which he re-leased the Archbishop of York and Lord Stanley.

As Richard's accession had been one of the most peaceful in the English annals, so his coronation ranks among the most mag-nificent. Many very minute particulars are preserved in the Heralds' College, also in the Harleian MSS., relative to the gorgeous ceremonial which took place on the 6th of July, 1483. Although low in stature, Richard III. is now generally allowed to have been ex-tremely handsome in face (as in the fine por-trait at Cossey Hall); as he rode in state from the City to Westminster, his rich dress would have concealed any defects in his figure. There he was met by almost the entire hierarchy, and by the Queen, who came "in gentle majesty with robes like the

King's, her train borne by the Countess of Richmond." They were crowned with great solemnity by the Archbishop of Canterbury; at the banquet which followed, "the Lady Richmond took precedence, not only of all other Countesses, but even of the Duchesses of Suffolk and of Buckingham" (though the latter was the King's own sister); while Lord Stanley, as Lord High Steward, served the King "with one dish of gold, and another of silver." Soon after, Richard made Stanley Constable of England and gave him the Garter; but, despite these marks of favour, the Countess's pleadings could never prevail with him to allow her son to return from exile, nor to restore his forfeited estates. Indeed, the liberation of Harry of Richmond did not commend itself to Richard III.; his first diplomatic move was the despatch of Sir Thomas Hutton to the Duke of Brittany, to renew the existing treaty, and ensure Richmond's continued imprisonment by sumptuous gifts — a mission accomplished so satisfactorily that all fears from that quarter were thought to be finally disposed of.

A few weeks later, the King having gratified his subjects by the announcement that a portion of the taxes due to him were spontaneously remitted, and that a large tract of land at Wildhouse, which King Edward had turned into a deer park, would be disforested, he and the Queen left Windsor on a Royal progress through the North of England. Their tour of state began at Reading ; thence they moved to Glastonbury and Tewkesbury (the scene of Richard's first battle), and on to Warwick, where the King received the answers of the Courts to whom he had announced his accession. The letter of Louis XI. was brief, but courteous ; the Duke of Burgundy wrote more cordially ; while the King and Queen of Spain were effusive in their congratulations. Whether the friendly greetings of his brother Monarchs raised his spirits, or the hearty acclamations he received from his subjects made Richard wish to drink more deeply still of the cup of popular enthusiasm, or from any other cause, the idea seems suddenly to have occurred to him, at Nottingham, of having the ceremony of coronation repeated at York.* That the city with which his family were connected by many ties, and which had been ever faithful to

* It has been suggested that there may have been some connection between the death of Richard's nephews and this suddenly conceived idea. Some strange sophistry might have led him to imagine that a subsequent coronation would consecrate his title ; for it is a legal maxim that accession to the crown removes all previous criminality.

their fortunes, might see him in the most exalted function of majesty, was no unnatural wish in a man so fond of display, and it was carried out with the utmost magnificence. The King and Queen appeared to the loyal people of York clad in their Royal robes, and Anne led by the hand her little son of ten years, now for the first time proclaimed Prince of Wales, wearing a demi-crown and the insignia of his Principality; whereupon the delighted citizens of the Northern capital, who had never witnessed such a scene since the days of the Heptarchy, shouted their rapturous applause.

But Fortune, that had hitherto so markedly befriended Richard's onward career, had bestowed her last gift: now began for him " the evil days which dog our delight"; now was heard the ominous tread of those wool-shodden feet that sometimes move so swiftly. Whether the assumption by Richard's son of the title of Prince of Wales recalled to people's memories the handsome, golden-haired lad who had borne it so many years, or whether some trifle, light as air, such as has often mysteriously led up to the revelation of a great crime, moved men's minds, it is certain that the fate of Edward IV.'s children—to which the nation had hitherto

been curiously indifferent—suddenly became
a matter of absorbing interest, especially in
the Southern and Western provinces. Meet-
ings were held in many places, and the suggestion made that the Queen's daughters
should be taken in disguise from Westminster Sanctuary and sent abroad, so that
if any harm came to the Princes it should
be avenged by the crown returning to their
sisters.

This design Richard met at once by
having the Abbey and its dependencies surrounded with fortifications, well manned by
trusty guards, to watch over all the ingress
and egress : a measure which, far from allay-
ing the excitement, caused it to be spread to
the metropolis. " What has become of the
poor children in the Tower? " was the question which met the King wherever he went,
and his silence inflamed the rising anger of
the people. Taken by surprise, and trusting
that the certainty of their death would ter-
minate the commotion, he caused the report
to be spread that they were no more. The
news was received with a burst of indignation and violent emotion, which portended
the most dangerous hostility. " In every
town, city, and public place crowds assem-
bled, openly wept, and piteously sobbed."*

* "Grafton's Chronicle," Vol. II., p. 119.

There was lamentation all throughout the land, as of Rachel weeping for her children ; every mother's heart beat in sympathy with the once unpopular and frivolous Queen of Edward IV. when it was told that on receiving the fatal tidings she fell senseless to the ground, and lay long apparently dead ; and how, as feeling and memory returned, she had called on her children by various tender names, as if they could hear her, and especially reproached herself for surrendering her little York ; and how, kneeling down, she had implored Heaven to avenge the treachery of the destroyer. Richard, so lately applauded and honoured, became henceforth abhorred ; " no man durst take his part." The Lancastrians, gathering courage, fanned the flame of popular indignation ; while those among the Yorkists who had been the late King's friends were now ready to cast their lot in with them rather than serve under one who had trampled on every law, human and divine ; new party connections were formed, in which the Countess of Richmond, who hitherto had abstained from all interference in political matters, took an important share.

It will be remembered that at the time of

Lord Stanley's release from the Tower—previous to Richard III.'s coronation—Morton, Bishop of Ely, was not set at liberty, but committed to the milder custody of the Duke of Buckingham, with whom, though carefully guarded, he was on the footing rather of a guest than of a prisoner. Some time elapsed before the Duke rejoined the Bishop at Brecon, and he was still to all appearance a loyal follower of Richard ; but in a private conversation—related with much detail by Sir Thomas More, as from Morton's lips—the Duke let fall some expressions which encouraged his companion to speak his own mind freely concerning "the late Protector, now called King, but who by his crimes had forfeited the right to govern so noble a realm as England. I dare affirm," he continued, "that if the Turk stood in competition with that killer of infants, the people of England would prefer him to Richard." Morton then went on to hint at a restoration of the House of Lancaster, with some uncertainty, whether real or feigned, as to who was actually its head ; hinting that if Buckingham himself stood in that position, he should lay claim to the crown ; or, in the other event, support the Prince he recognised, and put an end to all

81

dynastic disputes by marrying him to the Princess Elisabeth. "All evil," he concluded, "would then end, domestic discord would cease, and this noble realm enjoy the blessings of universal peace."

The Duke listened attentively, but made no answer, so that the Bishop grew alarmed, lest he had spoken too frankly for his own safety. At last Buckingham replied: "Fear nothing, my Lord, I will keep my word with you, that no man should hear anything we might say. To-morrow we will talk of the matter; let us now go to supper."

The next morning the Duke himself introduced the subject. Taking off his hat, he uttered a solemn prayer to God for the Commonweal of England, and then spoke unreservedly to the Bishop—admitting that his own feelings had been hostile to the late King, so that he had no care or wish that his sons should succeed him, and had willingly helped Richard in his ambitious schemes; exaggerating, rather than understating, his own share in the matter. "By my means, as you know well, Richard was made first Protector and then King:" Buckingham then went on to complain of Richard's ingratitude, in refusing him the confiscated lands of his ancestor, the Earl of Hereford, which should have been his by inheritance, but were retained by King Edward I. " I have borne his ingratitude," the Duke went on to say, " I concealed my resentment, I carried me outwardly fair ; but when I was certainly informed of the murder of the two innocent Princes (to which, God be my judge, I never consented), my blood curdled at his treason and barbarity." Buckingham then told how he had begun to consider how he could best deprive Richard of his Royal dignity ; he seems first to have contemplated claiming the crown in his own person, as lineal descendant, through his mother, from John, Earl of Somerset, and so from John of Gaunt. While pondering these things on his way from Worcester to Shrewsbury, he casually met the Countess of Richmond, who was proceeding on a visit of devotion to the Shrine of Our Lady of Worcester. They rode a while together, and the Countess took occasion to beseech him to intercede with the King on behalf of her son, Harry of Richmond, to whom she was desirous permission should be given to return to England, and put forward as a ground for her request the close tie of blood between them. These words of the Lady Margaret

83

recalled to Buckingham's memory what it seems strange he should have forgotten, that her claim as daughter of John, Duke of Somerset, was stronger than his own as a grandson of the same Duke's aunt. For the moment his disappointment was keen, and after answering the lady courteously he parted from her. In his lodging that night he revolved the matter, considering whether, as he could not claim the crown by birth, he might not gain it by election. Finally, he became convinced the project was hopeless, and determined to support the Earl of Richmond. This conclusion was heartily approved by Morton, who then asked who should first be applied to in so perilous an adventure. "The mother of Henry of Richmond," was Buckingham's reply. "Oh, if you begin there," answered Morton, "I have an old friend, Reginald Braye, whom I will send for to receive your Grace's commands." Bray, who was steward of the Countess of Richmond's household, was at once summoned to Brecon, and through him the Queen Dowager sounded as to the marriage of her daughter Elisabeth with the Earl of Richmond. She cordially approved, and the Countess of Richmond, on her son's part, accepted the terms proposed for the union of the two factions.

She then sent her own chaplain, Christopher Urswicke, to Brittany, to make known to Richmond all that had been agreed on. A little later a more important personage, Hugh Conway, followed with a considerable sum of money, and further assurances of the great love and favour the most part of the nobility bore towards him, and the loving hearts of the commonalty. Others went on their own account to Richmond, with entreaties to come over at once, and the 18th of October was fixed on for the intended rising. Some rumours having reached the King, Buckingham was summoned peremptorily to appear at Court : on his sending an equally haughty refusal, Richard at once threw all his energies into warlike preparations, and when the 18th October came, and Buckingham, as had been agreed, marched in open revolt from Brecon to Webly, the Royal force was ready to meet him. The elements were in Richard's favour ; torrents of rain fell for ten days without ceasing, making it impossible for Buckingham to cross the Severn. His followers, disheartened and frightened, fell away from him, and, without a blow being struck, he was taken prisoner, and, according to orders Richard had previously issued, immediately beheaded without a trial.

The King then marched quickly through the Western counties, where other risings were trampled out in blood, while the estates of those implicated were divided among the King's supporters or annexed to the Crown. Against the Countess of Richmond a special indictment was drawn up, accusing her of treason and treachery. Her estates were forfeited, but in consideration of Lord Stanley's services he was allowed to retain them for his life, with a strict injunction that "his wife was to be kept in some secret place at home, without any servant or company, so that from thenceforth she should never send letter or message to her son, nor to any of his friends or confederates, by which the King should be molested ' or troubled. Which command was forthwith put in execution, and accomplished according to his dreadful commandment."

Meanwhile, Harry of Richmond had not been inactive. During the last years of Edward IV.'s reign his durance had been somewhat less severe, and in the year following Richard's accession the King's jealousy was more excited against the Queen Dowager's friends than against the Lancastrians. A considerable degree of liberty was conceded to Richmond, which he was able to enjoy without molestation. He was much at the Court of Duke Francis, and there were even rumours of an engagement between him and the Duke's only daughter and heiress, Anne of Brittany.

But when his mother's messengers came, telling him that Buckingham was organising a rising in his favour, and that the hand of Elisabeth of York was offered him, all other projects were thrown to the winds. With the help of France and of Brittany, he hastily collected a force of five thousand fighting men, and sailed for the coast of Devon ; but a storm coming on, his ship was driven in the direction of Poole, close to the shore. Seeing the coast was lined with troops, he decided not to land till the rest of his fleet came up ; but sent a boat on shore to ask if the soldiers he saw were friends or enemies. The elusive answer came that they were stationed by Buckingham to receive him. But something in the manner of it excited suspicion, and Henry, weighing anchor, passed on to Plymouth, where he heard of Buckingham's failure and death. According to most historians, he returned at once to Brittany, while another version says that though he sent his fleet back to Vannes, Henry went secretly on shore by himself, and was for some weeks in hiding in Wales; and this is supported by much local tradition. A window is still shown at Talacre, out of which, when hard pressed by his pursuers, he is said to have leapt; and a tree marks a spot in the park whence he brought down with his crossbow a many-antlered stag.

In either case, Richmond had returned to Brittany before the year had ended, and thither he was followed by Richard's emissaries, who had orders to spare neither money nor effort to get him into their power. Duke Francis steadily refused to yield him up; but his treasurer, Peter Landois, formerly Richmond's friend, was now corrupted by Richard's bribes, and took advantage of an illness, which incapacitated the Duke for a time, to negotiate the captive's surrender. But Morton got warning of the affair, and sent the trusty Urswicke once more to Henry, to tell him of his danger. He, always prompt in action, took horse at once, and rode along byways into France, so keenly pursued that, though he had four days' start of his enemies, they reached the French frontier within an hour of his having crossed it. Richmond's cousin, Louis XI., was now dead, but Anne of Beaujeu, who, during her young brother's minority, acted as Regent, with the title of " Governess of France," was far more zealous for her young kinsman than her father had ever been. Already, when he first started to join Buckingham, she had procured him a contingent of four thousand soldiers and the loan of a considerable sum of money (Philip de Comines, p. 536). Now, on his return, notwithstanding the opposition of the Council of Regency, who were in favour of Richard III., she received him courteously, and continued, as far as was in her power, to favour his cause. Those of the leaders of Buckingham's rising who had effected their escape, came to join the Lancastrian standard, and on Christmas Day, 1483, Richmond and his adherents went in solemn state to the Cathedral of Reims, where, before the high altar, he pledged himself to the adherents of the House of York, that he would marry the Princess Elisabeth ; while they, taking the oath of allegiance to him, promised, on their side, never to cease warring against the usurper, Richard, till his destruction was effected.

It was, perhaps, the news of these proceedings, and the secession of many Yorkists which followed them, that induced Richard to summon Parliament, in January, 1484, to have the succession to the crown of England settled with more exactness, not only on the heirs of his body, but, failing them, on the children of his sister, the Duchess of Suffolk, to the exclusion of those of his elder brother, George, Duke of Clarence, as well as of the daughters of Edward IV. He then took measures to have the coast more carefully guarded, so as to prevent the landing again of Richmond, and dispersed spies throughout the kingdom, in order to gather information relative to persons suspected of favouring the Lancastrian cause. Many of these were thrown into prison, while all who had joined Richmond abroad were formally attainted, and their lands forfeited to the King's use.

Meanwhile, the sufferings of the refugees in Westminster Sanctuary had increased terribly in severity: soldiers stationed at every entrance watched day and night to prevent the access of their friends; and now that the Bishop of Salisbury, who had hitherto constantly visited them, to protect them from possible violence and supply their wants, was thrown into prison, their situation became pitiable. Deprived almost of the necessaries of life, seeing her daughters pining away before her eyes, the Queen Dowager, utterly broken in spirit, consented to leave the Sanctuary. She and her younger children were received with kindness by Queen Anne, while the Lady Elisabeth, whose great beauty and sweetness endeared her to all who came near her, was placed under the charge of her god-father, Lord Stanley, to whose care her father had, by his will, commended her. While at Derby House she was much in the company of her aunt, Queen Anne, who showed her almost sisterly affection, and at the Christmas festivities at Westminster treated her and her sister Cicely with marked distinction, although the fiction that their mother's marriage had been illegal, and consequently their condition illegitimate, had never been withdrawn.

But a grievous blow soon put an end to the hollow gaieties of Richard's Court : his only son, a promising boy of twelve, expired suddenly at Middleham Castle. Queen Anne, whose health had long been failing, was utterly prostrated by her affliction, and died, not, as has sometimes been said, by poison, but of a lingering disease which grief had aggravated. Left childless and a widower, Richard's ambition remained unchanged— the adverse blows of fate only made him cling with greater determination to power. He persisted in ignoring the claims of Clarence's children, again naming as his successor the son of his eldest sister,* and was universally believed to be bent on defeating the schemes of his opponents for the union of the Roses, by himself marrying his niece, the Princess Elisabeth. Baker, in his chronicle, says that, to the astonishment of all men, it was reported that the King had overcome the scruples of the Queen Dowager, who was said to have consented to an application to the Pope for the necessary dispensation.

The pitiable situation of this unhappy lady, deprived by death of her nearest kindred and of all on whose help or counsel she might have relied; in terror lest the committal of her daughters to the Tower might be the result of her refusal, left her scarcely a free agent, and justifies the charitable suggestion that her alleged consent was extorted by maternal fears,† and her scruples laid at rest by a confident expectation that neither the

° The young Earl of Lincoln, whom King Richard, in default of male heirs, thus procured to be nominated as his successor, was the fourth in descent from Philippa de Roet, the wife of Geoffrey Chaucer, the poet, and sister of Catherine, Lady Swynford, to whom Harry of Richmond stood in precisely the same relationship.

† Halsted, p. 137.

Holy See nor the English nation would consent to so revolting a union. And however much Elizabeth Woodville's demeanour lacked magnanimity, the result justified her prudence; for when the rumour that the King intended to marry his niece spread abroad, it was received with such indignation that, on the peremptory demand of his Council, Richard publicly disclaimed it, and sent the Lady Elisabeth to strict durance in the fortress of Sheriff's Hutton. But even the report had weakened Richard's hold on the nation : daily defections taught him to distrust even his personal adherents, and his temper was further exasperated by the knowledge that a powerful, almost brilliant, Court was gathering round Richmond. The delight he expressed on the news that his rival had sailed from Harfleur on the 7th August, 1485, was probably genuine ; action was the best ·anodyne to his fears and troubles. Quickly mustering his forces, he sent peremptory orders, coupled with fearful menaces in case of disobedience, to his subjects to join him, and fixed his head-quarters at Nottingham. Hither he summoned Lord Stanley, who answered that he could not come, as he was stricken with the sweating sickness ; however, a few days later Stanley moved slowly eastward as far as Leicester, where he was to await the King. It was on the night before the battle of Bosworth that the interview between Stanley and Richmond, of which Shakespeare makes so dramatic a use, is said to have taken place:

RICHMOND : All comfort that the dark night can afford
   Be to thy person, noble father-in-law !
   Tell me, how fares our loving mother ?
STANLEY : I, by attorney, bless thee for thy mother,
   Who prays continually for Richmond's good.
                    Richard III., Act v., Scene 3.

When morning dawned Richard called his supporters together, and in a short, energetic speech expressed his regret for the one criminal action which sullied his name ; then, after dwelling on Richmond's inexperience and the weakness of his army, exhorted his own followers to the victory that lay so easily within their reach : " Wherefore, advance your standards, let each man give but one sure stroke, and the day is ours. As for myself, I do assure you, that I will this day either triumph by victory or suffer death for immortal fame."

Richmond, meanwhile, rode from rank to rank through his army, giving comfortable words to all : then ascending a small knoll, armed in all pieces but his helmet, he addressed the whole line. He was in the twenty-seventh year of his age, not much above middle height, but strong and well-proportioned : his countenance was lively, his yellow hair shone like burnished gold, and his grey eyes sparkled with the joy of battle. In a loud, clear voice, and with easy eloquence, he conveyed his indignant exposition of Richard's cruelty, his intimation that it is not numbers that give success, his own trust in Heaven for victory, his pledge that in such a quarrel he would rather die than fail them, rather be a corpse than a prisoner. He finally appealed confidently to Heaven for triumph, for had they not come to avenge the shedding of innocent blood? " Get this day, and be conquerors ; lose it, and be slaves. In the name of the Supreme and of St. George, let every man advance forth his standard."*

Richard's army was far the more numerous ; the Duke of Norfolk, the Lords Surrey, Ferrers, and Ayton fought valiantly for him, but the Stanleys stood sullenly aloof. Seeing this, Richard sent Lord Stanley word his son, Lord Strange, should be slain before his eyes. " Tell King Richard," was Stanley's answer, " that the Lord of the

* " Grafton's Chronicle," Vol. II., p. 153.

Isle of Man has other sons alive." Stung
to the quick, Richard, leaving the post of
command, in which he was well protected,
rushed down the hill towards the enemy's
lines, challenging Richmond, and, followed
only by a few devoted adherents, dashed
through the ranks with a vehemence nothing
could withstand, making his way almost to
the spot where his rival stood. With his
own hand he slew Sir William Brandon,*
and unhorsed Sir John Cheney, till, over-
powered by numbers, weakened by loss of
blood, "in battle and not in flight," writes
the Monk of Croyland, "stricken with many
wounds, Richard fell on the field of battle,
like a courageous and most daring Prince.
And many a noble knight lost his life that
day, fighting for Richard the King."

* The weird, withered arm, described by More and
Shakespeare :
"Behold mine arm,
Is like a blasted sapling, withered up,"
could never have dealt such strokes. Nor is the line,
"A horse, a horse! My kingdom for a horse!"
true to history, for the Harleian MSS. say : "Then came a
knight and brought him a fresh horse, saying : 'It is right
time for ye to flye, here is thy horse ; another day ye may
fight worthily again.' To whom Richard replied : 'Not
one foot will I fly, so long as breath bides within my breast.
For by Him that shapeth both sea and land, this day shall
end my battles or my life. I will die King of England.'"

CHAPTER V.

HARDLY had the shout which proclaimed Harry of Richmond victor died away than he, "as one that had been bred under a pious mother, and was in his nature a great observer of religious forms, caused the *Te Deum laudamus* to be solemnly sung in the presence of the whole army upon the plain, while kneeling down he thanked God for the victory he had gained."* Then, after giving directions that the wounded on both sides should be carefully tended, he rode on to Leicester, where, according to tradition, he tarried a day in his mother's company. Between Bosworth and London Henry had, Lord Bacon holds, a knotty point to decide ; whether he would claim the crown of England by conquest, by marriage with Elisabeth of York, or by inheritance. Many writers assume that Henry had not a shadow of hereditary right—almost all favour the title of the House of York—it is, as Bishop Stubbs rather sarcastically remarks, one of

* "Bacon's History of Henry VII."

97

H

the few points on which the extremists on both sides, Conservative and Radical, agree : Edward IV. was heir-general to Edward III., therefore he pleases the Conservatives ; he came to the throne by a revolution, and thus satisfies their opponents. But it is forgotten that in the fifteenth century the analogy on which the succession to the throne rested was still a debatable matter : Henry I. had tried to fix it in the female line, civil war had ensued, and the crown was kept by Stephen. The claim of the House of Lancaster to represent the male line of descent from Edward III. was incontestable ; their assumption of the crown had been supported by a Parliamentary title, and strengthened by sixty years of possession. With regard to the question of legitimacy, the validity of the legitimation of the Beauforts by King, Pope, and Parliament, would certainly not have been questioned by any of their descendants. Further (though this claim was never put forward), Bishop Stubbs remarks that if the Royal succession follows the analogy of a private estate, then Henry VII., as the nearest kinsman to Henry VI., had a claim to succeed on that ground. If that claim, it might be said, was barred by half-blood : the answer is that the doctrine

of half-blood does not affect the Royal succession. At any rate, if Henry VII.'s claim
does not now satisfy either the Legitimists
or the Progressists, it certainly sátisfied
himself. Again, to quote Lord Bacon : "The
King, out of the greatness of his mind,
presently cast the die, and preferring his
affection to his own line and blood, and
liking best that title which made him independent, and being in his nature and
constitution not very apprehensive or fore-
casting of events far off, but an entertainer
of fortune by the day, resolved to rest upon
the line of Lancaster by the main and to use
the other two—that of marriage and that
of battle—but as supporters ; the one to
appease secret discontents, and the other
to set down open murmur and dispute.
Whereupon the King, presently, that very
day, being the 22nd of August, 1484,
assumed the style of King in his own
name, without mention of Lady Elisabeth
at all, and set forth by easy journeys to
the City of London, receiving the acclamations and applause of the people as he went :
which were indeed true and unfeigned, for
they thought generally that he was a Prince
as ordained and sent from Heaven to unite
and put an end to the strife between the two

houses, which, although they had in the times
of Henry IV. and a part of Henry VI., on
the one side, and the times of Edward IV.
on the other, lucid intervals and happy
pauses, yet they did ever hang over the
kingdoms, ready to break forth into new per-
turbations and calamities." On the eighth
day from the battle of Bosworth, which was
a Saturday, and which he chose to account
a day propitious to him, King Henry, having been met by the Lord Mayor and City
Companies at Shoreditch, rode amid much
state and rejoicing into London, alighting
first at St. Paul's Cathedral, where he
offered the three standards that had been
carried before him in battle, the banner of
St. George, that of the Dun Cow, and the
banner of Arthur Pendragon—a fiery dragon
on a green ground ; which, fulfilling the prophecy of the Welsh bard Taliesin, had borne
down the Leopard. And by the King's
order, the Royal herald, *Blanc Sanglier*,
after he had officiated at the interment of
Richard III., changed his name to *Rouge
Dragon*, as the especial cognisance of the
House of Tudor.

Henry VII.'s first Parliament met on September 1st, when the King took occasion
more clearly to assert the view he held, and

had made known by his deeds, that his title
to the throne rested on hereditary right—
sanctioned and confirmed by the award of
the Lord of Hosts. Then Parliament, after
granting a subsidy so generous that it made
the King practically independent for several
years [it was deemed prudent to add a
note that it was not to count as a precedent in the case of future Monarchs],
declared that the succession to the crown
lay in King Henry, in the heirs of
his body, and in none other ; and pro-
ceeded to reverse the attainders of his partisans. With respect to his mother, the
Lady Margaret, a special enactment was
made, restoring to her all her honours and
possessions, for her absolute and personal
use. Henry's next act was to reward the
friends, kinsmen,- and servitors, of all grades
and classes, who had been faithful to him
in his adversities. Lord Stanley was made
High Chancellor of England and Earl of
Derby ; Jasper, Earl of Pembroke, created
Duke of Bedford ; Bishop Morton became
Lord Chancellor, and a little later was promoted to the See of Canterbury. Christopher Urswicke, the Lady Margaret's faithful
messenger, promoted to be Dean of York
and King's Almoner ; while Reginald Bray

was attached to his person as Privy Coun-
cillor. An amnesty was proclaimed, from
which only a few were excepted, and
the rejoicings would have been complete
but for the sudden outbreak of the epidemic known as the sweating sickness.

It was said, though it can be hardly
credited, that among those first attacked
scarce one in a hundred recovered ; and
being extremely contagious, the disease
spread with great rapidity, especially among
the higher classes : in the space of six weeks
two Lords Mayors and several Aldermen of
London were among the victims. However,
by the middle of October the epidemic,
though still spreading throughout the country, was dying out in London, and the
King's coronation, which had been deferred
for a time, was now fixed for the 31st of the
month. On the preceding day the King,
having dined with the Archbishop of Canterbury, rode at the head of a splendid escort
over London Bridge to the Tower, where
he was received by the Lord Mayor and
City Guilds. The coronation at Westminster
Abbey took place with all due pomp and
ceremony, the Earl of Richmond officiating
as Lord High Constable. Of the Countess,
Bishop Fisher tells that " when she saw her

son the King crowned in all that great triumph and glory, she wept marvellously, giving as the reason that she never was yet in that prosperity, but the greater it was the more she dreaded adversity." But tears well up from unexpected sources, and who can wonder at Margaret Beaufort's emotion at a scene which must have recalled to her the far-away prophecy of Henry VI.—now venerated by all the common people as a Saint —made when her son was but an Eton schoolboy ; the troubles that so quickly followed ; his hurried flight into Brittany ; his long exile ; the sufferings and privations from which all her love and anxiety could not save him ; then his desperate and, at first, apparently unsuccessful venture ; the time when he was a fugitive in Wales, hunted like a partridge on the hills by the most merciless and vindictive Monarch that ever wore the crown of England ; then his second coming : the agonising suspense, the swift and glorious victory. And now he stood before her in the pride and glory of his manhood ; still dutiful and loving, gladly acknowledging himself " more deeply indebted to her than ever was son to mother."

Three months later Westminster Abbey saw another great function, at which the

King's mother shed no tears, but shared the universal jubilation. Henry had been deeply chagrined and offended by the report of Elisabeth of York's possible marriage with her uncle, Richard III., while her troth was still plighted to him ; and by the Queen, Dowager's double dealing ; and had retorted by entering into projects of marriage first with the heiress of Brittany, and later with the Lady Maud Herbert. But whether the pretty story known as " Lady Bessie's Lament," told in verse by Brereton, of Elisabeth's sending Henry, by the help of Lord Stanley, a ring and loving message, assuring him of her fidelity, be true or not, it is certain that, after his victory at Bosworth, Henry treated the Princess Elisabeth with the highest consideration. The day following the battle he sent an escort, commanded by Sir Robert Willoughby, to bring her from Sheriff - Hutton, where Richard had placed her in strict durance, to her mother's house at Westminster, with all honour and courtesy. During the weeks that ensued it is said that the Princess suffered from much doubt and anxiety as to the King's further intentions ; but it was an important part of his policy that his title to the crown should be fully and distinctly recognised, without any dependence on his future wife's Yorkist claim. Once this was done, the preparations for the marriage began without further delay, to the great joy of the people, to whom Elisabeth's youth, grace, and beauty, her generous and gentle disposition, her cruel misfortunes, and the patience with which she had borne them, endeared her.

So that when, on the prorogation of Parliament, the Lord Chancellor announced that before it reassembled the marriage of the King with Princess Elisabeth would take place, public rejoicings were unbounded. A tournament was proclaimed, and great preparations made for the nuptials, which were celebrated on January 20th, 1486, "with all possible religious and glorious magnificence at Court, and by the people with bonfires, dancings, songs, and banquets." In the marriage procession, "each partisan of the Lancastrian House gave his hand to a lady of the Yorkist party, she holding a bouquet (though the season was mid-winter!) of the red and white roses combined." King Henry, then in his twenty-seventh year, with the handsome, well-favoured face the people acclaimed; Elisabeth, tall and stately, the beauty of regular, delicate features enhanced by the fair complexion and brilliant colour-

ing which was the personal attribute of so
many of her descendants, must have made a
handsome couple as they stood before Bourchier, Archbishop of York, "who by his
hand held the sweet posie whereon the red
and white roses were bound together." Immediately after was celebrated the wedding
of Princess Cicely, the Queen's sister, with
Leo, Lord Welles, son of the late Duchess
of Somerset, and so half-brother to the Countess of Richmond. And, finally, the brave
old soldier, Jasper Tudor, now Duke of Bedford, led to the altar the twice widowed
Duchess of Buckingham, sister to the Dowager Queen, Elisabeth Woodville. When the
festivities were ended the Court moved to
Winchester, and in Lent the King started
alone on a progress through the Northern
counties. On the road to Lincoln he had
to suppress a dangerous insurrection; however, by Easter Day York was safely
reached, and that city, once the stronghold
of the rival house, and especially devoted
to Richard III., now greeted his successor
with cries of: "King Harry! King Harry!
The Lord bless that sweet and well-favoured
face!" From York Henry returned to Winchester, to be greeted by his wife, and by his
mother, who had borne her company, with
sincerer joy.

In accordance with the King's wishes, the Court remained through the summer at Winchester, in order that the expected heir to the throne might be born in the Castle which, according to tradition, had been originally built by King Arthur; and, by Henry's desire, the Countess of Richmond drew up an ordinance relative to the preparations and etiquette to be observed, according to ancient customs, at the accouchement of the Queens of England, but which she wisely modified by frequent insertions of the phrase "as it may please Her Majesty," "Her Highness' pleasure being understood as to what chamber it may please her to be delivered in, the same be hung with rich cloth of arras, sides, roof, windows and all, except one window, which must be hanged so that she have light when it pleases her." The taking to chamber was a ceremonious function, almost a religious rite. A solemn Mass was said, at which the Queen received Communion, afterwards proceeding in great state to her apartments. When she had reached them, she tarried a time in the anteroom. when a "voyde of refreshments" was served; that done, the Queen bade farewell to her lords and officers, and entered her chamber, where she was waited on only by her own sex — in the Lady Margaret's words : " Women were to be made all manner of officers, butlers, sewers, and pages ; receiving all needful things at the chamber door." Among sundry quaint preparations is enjoined " a little cradle of tree, of a yard and a quarter long, and twenty-two inches broad, in a frame set forth by painter's craft, superbly furnished with cloth of gold, ermyne fur, and crimson velute." At its baptism the infant was to be provided with a little taper to carry in its hand to the altar, to be lit when the baptism was concluded : then the infant presented the lighted taper, and a thank-offering was made " as it may please the King to appoint ": after which the child was to be confirmed. The Countess seems to have remained with her daughter-in-law during the ceremony ; but her husband, the Earl of Derby, who was one of the god-fathers, was present and gave the Royal infant a rich salt-cellar of gold.

The year following the birth of the Countess of Richmond's first grandchild was troubled by the strange rebellion headed by Lambert Simnel. However, it was quelled before the autumn, and Henry, finding his rival too low-born and uneducated to be considered responsible, good-naturedly forgave him, making him a scullion in the Royal kitchen. This act of grace was in honour of Elisabeth's coronation, which had been long deferred, but was to exceed in splendour all previous pageants. On the Friday preceding the Queen went by water from Greenwich, royally accompanied ; the barges of the great City Companies coming out to meet her. The barge of the Lincoln's Inn students surpassed all the others : " Therein was a great red dragon " (in honour of the Arthurian descent of the House of Tudor), "spouting flames of fire into the Thames, and many other gentlemanly pageants, well devised, to do Her Highness sport and pleasure withal. When the Queen landed at the Tower, the King's Highness welcomed her in such a manner and form as was to all the estates a very goodly sight, and right joyous and comfortable to behold." On the next day, being Saturday, Elisabeth set forth again from the Tower on her procession through the City to Westminster Palace, magnificently arrayed, "her fair yellow hair hanging at length down her back." She was preceded by four baronesses, riding palfreys, and by Jasper Tudor, as Grand Steward. Her old friend, Stanley, now Earl of Derby, with the Earl of Oxford, attended her to her rich open litter, four Knights of the Bath bearing a canopy over her head while the citizens hung velvets and cloth of gold from the windows, and stationed children dressed like angels to sing the Queen's praises as she passed. During the coronation the King, who wished that Elisabeth should alone receive the people's homage, ensconced himself in a closely-latticed tribune, between the altar and pulpit in Westminster Abbey, whence, with his lady mother, he watched the ceremony. And again at the stately banquet prepared in Westminster Hall, these two were in a recess placed in one of the upper windows, while the Queen sat at the head of the table below, served by her own ladies: after which Elisabeth departed "with God's blessing, and the rejoicing of many a true Englishman's heart."

But on the next day, when the Queen still kept her estate (sat in Royal state under a canopy), the Countess of Richmond was seated at her right, and in the time of feasting that followed was scarcely ever separated from her daughter-in-law.

The Christmas of 1487 was observed by the Court with great state at Greenwich Palace ; the Lady Margaret was present, and was thrice cried largesse by the herald in these terms : " Du hault puissant et ex-

cellente princesse la mère du roi notre sove-
raigne, comtesse de Richmond et de Derbye,
largesse." Her gift to the heralds, according
to one account, was twenty shillings ; another
makes it a little more. The Earl of Derby,
who was also present, was cried largesse as
" Beaupère du roi notre souverain." On
Twelfth Day the Countess wore a "like
mantell and surcot with the Queen, with a
rich coronal on her head."

During the year 1488 the Countess of
Richmond seems to have resided much at
Court, for she is mentioned as having been
present with the King and Queen at the
celebration of the principal festivals. She
was at Windsor for Easter, and on the
Feast of St. George she and the Queen
were clothed in gowns of the Garter,
similar to those worn by the Sovereign
and Knights of the Order, and at the
chanting of the *Te Deum* the Countess
was censed next after the King and
Queen and before the Knights Companions.
On the Sunday following she and the Queen
being arrayed in gowns of the livery of the
Order, rode to Evensong in a splendid chair
covered with cloth of gold and drawn by six
coursers trapped in the same manner, and
followed by a suite of twenty-one ladies clad

in crimson velvet and riding on palfreys superbly ornamented. To these details of dress some antiquarian interest attaches, as it has been inaccurately said that after the reign of Edward IV. there was no instance of ladies wearing the livery of the Garter.

The position filled by the "King's Mother," as, from the time of her son's accession, the Countess of Richmond was affectionately called, was in many ways exceptional. Henry VII.'s claim to the throne was through her, yet based on the favouring of the male before the female line of descent, and of the exclusion of women from sovereign power ; while she, though always anxious to put prominently forward her dutiful loyalty to her dearly beloved son and Sovereign, was yet of vigorous active nature, which delighted in every opportunity of doing good that her rank and station afforded.

· However, the social relations of the time made it easy for the Countess of Richmond to take a prominent part in public affairs without overstepping the limits imposed by her sex and position ; for all through the Middle Ages women had a considerable and uncontested share in the serious business of life. In feudal times, high-born ladies were often, in the frequent absences of their lords on crusades or other expeditions, left as custodians of the family possessions, and had then shown that their sex did not unfit them for positions of great responsibility, needing courage, readiness, and resource. Even when manners had become gentler the old tradition lived on ; while in the middle and lower classes women carried on business in a number of crafts from which they have been in later times practically excluded, and were ad-- mitted to many more of the privileges of ·citizenship. This is shown by the records of the numerous merchant and trade guilds, which did so much to mould and ennoble the lives of burgesses and artisans, making them feel that something higher than personal gain and material enjoyment should be the aim of life. These, almost without exception, were formed pretty equally of men and women, all aiding one another in law-abiding liberty and charity, and exercising a more enduring influence on public affairs than has hitherto been achieved by any modern political organisation, withal doing much to soften the social inequalities so marked in those days. There is, for instance, an entry in the book of the Guild of St. Katherine, Stamford, showing that the King's mother and one of her servants, named Richard Cotimont, were admitted to membership on the same day.

Almost the first work to which the Countess of Richmond put her hand seems to have been an attempt to reclaim Hatfield Chase, which was the portion belonging to her of the all but limitless swamp, generally known as the Great Fen, which then covered a considerable part of Cambridgeshire, Huntingdon, and Lincoln counties, All these "drowned lands," as they were called, formed by the overflow of the Trent, Ouse, Don, and their affluents, contained immense quantities of fish and game ; venison and rabbits were plentiful even in the cottages of the poor; beavers, otters, martens, and other animals valuable for their fur abounded ; and off the tract of heather, from which Hatfield (or Heathfield) derives its name, turf could be cut for fuel in large quantities, and was much preferred by the well-to-do dwellers in the cities, to "that noxious and noisome mineral, coal." So that the value of the fen was much greater* than that of an equal quantity of solid land. But these marshy waters were a continual source of fever and

* Denton's "England in the Fifteenth Century."

ague to the surrounding inhabitants. To reclaim them (as had been done to some extent by colonies of monks, whose great foundations of Ely, Wisbeach, Croyland, and Peterborough rose up like oases in the dreary waste) and fit them for the habitation of Christian folk, was accounted a pre-eminently good work ; and in undertaking it, the Countess of Richmond was probably stimulated by the advice and example of her friend, Archbishop Morton, who was doing it on a much larger scale, and with conspicuous success; the great drain he cut between Wisbeach and Peterborough still exists in good working order, and is known as Morton's Leam. But neither Hatfield Chase nor the southern portion of the Great Fen were thoroughly reclaimed until Charles I., to whom the Countess of Richmond's estates had descended, took up the work in earnest, and got over a famous engineer from Holland, Cornelius Vermuyden, whose experience enabled him to cope with what had been thought insurmountable difficulties.

In August, 1486, the King gave his mother the wardship of the two sons of the late Duke of Buckingham (who, it will be remembered, was beheaded in 1483, by order of Richard III.), together with the

custody of their estates. The management
of the vast possessions of the House of
Buckingham was no slight trust, but it
seems to have been well attended to, as
the young Duke, when he reached manhood, was one of the richest nobles at the
Court of Henry VII. Giustiani, the Venetian Ambassador, estimated his annual reve-
nues at thirty thousand ducats—which Mr.
Denton calculates would amount to one
hundred and twenty thousand pounds a
year of our money (Denton's " England
in the Fifteenth Century," p. 266). It
would be difficult at the present day to
name an instance of the sole wardship
of a minor, with such large interests
involved, being given to a lady. Beside the Duke of Buckingham and his
brother, other young men of distinction
were brought up in the Countess of Richmond's household. In 1493 she addressed
a letter to the Chancellor and Regents of
the University of Oxford, asking them to
permit the absence of Maurice Westbury
from the University, as he was retained
by her for the instruction of " certain
young men of her finding." Cooper thinks
(though he does not, as is usual with him,
give his authority) that one of these young

men was the eldest son of the Earl of North-
umberland. The custom of bringing up
youths in the households of persons of distinction, which began in feudal times, seems
to have continued longer in England than
elsewhere ; the author of the " Italian Relation," alluding to it in 1488 as of something not usual in his own country. Yet,
as late as 1612, the Earl of Arundel wrote a
special instruction for his son William, telling
him how to behave himself in the household
of the Bishop of Norwich, " whom you are
to obey, as you do your parents or your
grandmother of Arundel, and in all things
esteem yourself as my lord's page ; a breeding which youths of my house, far superior
to yourself, were accustomed to." From the
beautiful account More has given us of his
own upbringing in the household of Archbishop Morton we gain some idea of what
the life of youths under the Lady Margaret's care might have been. And re-
proof, if needed, would have been kindly
but firmly 'administered, for gentle and
courteous as this noble lady was, she
could, when occasion required it, express
herself peremptorily. This may be seen
by a letter she wrote to the Mayor of
Coventry, the precise date of which does
not appear.

" By the King's Mother.

" Trusty and well-beloved, we greet you well. And whereas we of late, upon the complaint of one Owen, burgess of the city there, addressed other letters to you, and willed you by the same, and in our name, to call before you the parties comprised in the complaint and thereupon to order the variance depending betwixt them according to good conscience ; albeit as it is said, the said Owen can or may have no reasonable answer of you in that behalf, to our marvel. Wherefore we, in the King's name, command you eftsones to call before you the said parties, and roundly to examine them, and thereupon to order and determine the premises, as may stand with good reason and the equity of the King's laws : so as no complaint be made to us hereafter in that behalf : endeavouring you thus to do, as ye tender the King's pleasure.—M. Ri."

In upholding her own just rights, or those she held in trust for others, the King's mother was without fear or favour : notwithstanding her devoted attachment to the Church, she carried on many lawsuits against religious persons or corporations. In Easter Term, 1501, a suit which had been going on five years between her and the Dean of

Windsor was given in her favour : while two successive Abbots of Peterborough succeeded in recovering from her for their convents, after long and expensive litigation, the service of five knights' fees, fee farm grants and rent charges she or her predecessors had become unfairly possessed of. A suit was also brought by her against the Prior of Tunbridge, of which the result does not appear ; but after "an inquisition made at the suit of the King's mother" it was found that Royal rights had been suffered to lapse in the lordship of Corfe—much pasture and grazing land and rabbits warren lay in abeyance, and that the Abbess of Shaftesbury had appropriated the presentation of the parish church of Corfe Castle. As the jury found "that they were ignorant of the right of the Abbess thereto," it is probable the pious lady had to give it up.

For a woman to preside in a court of justice would not have caused any surprise in mediæval times. Even as late as the reign of Queen Mary Lady Berkeley was Justice of the Peace for Gloucestershire ; however, whether the Countess of Richmond actually held the commission is an open question ; Callis and Atkins, two eminent lawyers of the seventeenth century, are quoted as having stated it authoritatively; while Noy, the famous Attorney-General of Charles I., said that "he had made many an honest search for the commission by which she was appointed, but could never find it," though, he added, "he had seen many appointments made by her" ("Cooper's Memoir," p. 79).

But that she interested herself in the fair administration of justice is shown by Bishop Fisher's reference to her conduct in his "Mornynge Remembrance": "For the suitors it is not unknown how studiously she procured justice to be administered by a long season, so long as she was suffered, and of her own charge provided men learned for the purpose, evenly and indifferently to hear all causes and administer right and justice to every party, which were in no small number, yet meat and drink were denied to none of them." This suggests that the Countess may have exercised her privilege as lady of the manor, to hold courts of justice in her mansions, but that she engaged skilled lawyers to preside over them in her stead. And by the phrase, "as long as she was suffered," Bishop Fisher may have wished discreetly to convey that his patroness was not to be considered responsible for the severe and harsh legal measures with which, in the last years of her son's reign, Dudley and Empson are associated; for the designation which best suited this illustrious lady was that of peace-maker. The share she had in bringing about the reconciliation of the Roses, in allusion to which she was extolled by the contemporary poet, Daniel, as the "Mother, author, plotter, counsellor, of union," seemed to make this her special office, and for this her help and counsel were often solicited. As, for instance, great variances having arisen between the inhabitants of Kesteven and those of Holland, in the county of Lincoln, the Countess, who, at her mother's death had become possessed of the neighbouring manor of Deeping, procured a commission to be issued for the termination of the controversy, and the inquisition, which seems to have ended it happily, was sealed by her.

A little later a more serious dispute prevailed at Cambridge between the University and the Corporation, occasioned by conflicting claims to jurisdiction, and aggravated by mutual complaints of extortion and oppression of all kinds. To put an end to them, the contending parties had recourse to the King's mother, as one possessing the confidence and esteem of both. They besought her to cause the titles of either party to be examined, and the differences between them determined according to justice and good conscience. Upon this, she to use the language of the record, "intending the increase of cunning (knowledge), virtue, and Christian faith which is continued and increased by quiet study and learning of the laws of Almighty God, and also for the wealth and quietness and increase of the Mayor, burgesses, and bailiffs," required them to name arbitrators, on which they agreed, and on their giving mutual bonds to abide by such award as might be made, the arbitrators examined into the case ; the Countess being occasionally present, and, the award being made, she confirmed it with her seal. Afterwards the substance thereof was embodied in a formal indenture containing no less than thirty articles, the two last of which provided " that all future disputes and ambiguities should be referred to the Countess during her life, and after her death to the Lord Chancellor and the Lord High Treasurer of England." The effect of the composition is said to have been that the parties afterwards "lived at better peace to the great benefit of themselves, and of the whole realm besides."

To the gratitude of the University towards

the King's mother for her mediation, a quaint letter bears witness :

" Pleaseth it your noble Grace, most excellent Princess, our special good lady and singular benefactress. That forasmuch as not only heretofore ye have many and great benefits exhibited unto us, mercifully always condescending to our necessities, but also cease not daily by heaping benefits upon benefits, and adding bounteousness unto bounteousness to confer more and more upon us, your poor scholars, as witnesseth neither small nor few your gracious memorials here among us, besides your sundry labours, great pains, and large expenses taken and made oftentimes for us, and for the expedition and redressing many of our causes and businesses with other certain deeds which godly ye daily enterprise to the manifold praise of God and your own great merit. Where also ye so generously tender the restfulness of us all that for the more quietous setting of ourselves to virtue and learning ye will us to appoint and certify your Grace of such articles in the composition between ourselves and the town as we think ourselves aggrieved with. According to the which your gracious commandement we shall with all diligence apply ourselves, beseeching your Highness to see good direction and due reformation be made. We, our most gracious and beneficial Princess, upon humble and reverend consideration of these premises could not at this time contain but to use our tongues and pens, to signify the vehemence of our joy and entire hearty pleasing, not causeless in us conceived of your generousness, and that when we have done what we can for your noble Grace by means of our powers or otherwise, yet shall we unfeignedly do much less than we are bound to do, as knoweth the blessed Saints, whom we most humble beseech graciously to preserve you and everlastingly with the crown of most glory and joy to reward your goodness unto us ministered. Amen!"

Of the Lady Margaret's charitable foundations at this period of her life, the first recorded is the erection of an almshouse for poor women in the almonry of Westminster, near the old Chapel of St. Anne. This, in the reign of Henry VIII., was converted into a lodging for the singing men of the college.

At Sampford Peverell she enlarged the village church, one aisle of which is specially attributed to her. The painted glass window has her arms and those of the

Earl of Derby, with the inscription : " Mater Regis et Thome comitis Derbie maritus ejusdem Margaret."

Mr. Cooper thinks she was also a benefectress of the church of Dedham, in Essex, as her statue was placed at the east side of the battlements and her coronets all round.

The beautiful little Gothic building over St. Winifred's Well in Flintshire is said by Bingley to have been erected by the Countess of Richmond, though an older date is more frequently assigned to it. Pennant says the structure rose from the piety of the House of Stanley, and that the sculptures at the intersection of the arches are memorials of its benefactress. He adds : " There are besides some marks of illustrious donors ; for example, the profile of Margaret, mother to Henry VII., and that of her husband, the Earl of Derby, cut in the same stone."

In December, 1496, and March, 1497, the King granted his mother licences by which she was empowered to found two perpetual readers in holy theology : one in the University of Cambridge, and the other in Oxford, and to grant to each lands not exceeding twenty pounds per annum. Some delay took place in the endowment of these readerships (or lectureships as they are now termed), but it is probable that the office itself was soon filled. In Oxford, at any rate, Edmund Wylford, B.D., Fellow of Oriel (who had been recommended to her by the University through Archbishop Morton, their Chancellor), began to read "the quodlibets of the subtle doctor in the public schools of the University," as early as Trinity Term, 1497, and in the accounts of the University of Cambridge for 1498-9 are items relating to it.

On the last day of December, 1496, a deed was executed by which the Countess provided endowment for a Mass to be said daily at the Shrine of St. Edward " as long as the world shall endure, for her good estate during life, and for her soul after death." It was further stipulated that on each of the seven days of the week a particular Mass should be said : on Sunday, the Mass of the Holy Trinity ; on Monday, the Mass of *Requiem;* on Tuesday, the Mass of St. Edward ; on Wednesday, the Mass of the Holy Ghost ; on Thursday, the Mass of Corpus Christi ; on Friday, the Mass of the Five Wounds of Christ ; and on Saturday, the Mass of Our Lady. About the same time, or not long afterwards, she obtained licence from her son to settle lands of the annual value of ten pounds, for the endowment at Wimborne (where her father and mother were buried) of a perpetual chantry of one priest in honour of the Blessed Jesus and the Annunciation of the Blessed Virgin, and for the health of her soul and the souls of her parents : such priest " to teach grammar freely to all them that will to come thereunto."

CHAPTER VI.

THE Feast of All Hallows, 1488, was kept by the Countess of Richmond at Windsor, with the King and Queen ; she seems then to have accompanied them to London, as she was present shortly after at St. Paul's Cathedral, on the occasion of the solemn presentation to the King of a hallowed sword and cap of maintenance, which had been sent him by Pope Innocent VIII., and which were received with much ceremonial, having been brought in procession from Canterbury to London, where the bearers were welcomed by the Mayor and Aldermen "in their formalities, and all the craftes in their clothing."

At the Christmas Court festivities of the same year we again find the Countess with her son and daughter-in-law at Sheen, in Surrey. For this residence Henry VII. had a special affection ; and when the old Palace was destroyed by fire he rebuilt it, and gave the new Palace the name of Richmond, in memory of his ancestral home in Normandy, now no longer an English possession. However, Colyweston was the usual residence of the Earl of Derby and his Countess at this period, and there they kept much state ; she having her own Chancellor, Chamberlain, and Controller of the household, as became the King's mother, and largely exercising the kindly and thoughtful hospitality that was one of her most noted characteristics.

A familiar letter to the Queen's Chamberlain, Lord Ormond, is still extant, apparently written when the latter was abroad, in acknowledgment of a present he had made the Countess of a pair of gloves, which were too large for her hand : this, she intimates, with a touch of humour, may have arisen from the ladies of the country where he then was, being as large in their persons as they were elevated in rank.

" My Lord Chamberlain,

"I thank you heartily that you list so soon remember me with my gloves, the which were right good save they were too much for my hand. I think the ladies of that part be great ladyes, and according to their estate have great persons.

"As for news, I am sure you have more

than I can send you. Blessed be God, the King and Queen and all our sweet children be in good health. The Queen hath been a little crased (ill), but now is well, God be thanked, though her sickness is not so good as I would, but I trust hartily it shall be with God's grace ; whom I pray give you good speed in your great matters and bring you well and soon home.

" Written at Sheen, the 23rd day of April.

" M. RYCHEMOUND.

" To my Lord, Queen's Chamberlain."

It would seem to be about this time that the King's mother was entertained at Cressy Hall, near Surflet, in Lincolnshire, the seat of the Herons. The bed on which she lay had, in Dr. Stukely's time, been removed to a farmhouse by the fen side, called Wrigbolt ; where the doctor saw it : he describes it as ˎ " a very old-fashioned bed, with panels of embossed work, like many we see in old country houses."

In September, 1489, occurs a notice of the first visit made by the Lady Margaret to the city of Cambridge, with which her name has become so specially associated, in the quaint form of an allowance in the accounts

of the Corporation for payment made : " Six
pounds of comfits given to the mother of
the Lord the King, 6s. 8d.; and one flagon
of ipocras given to the same, 3s. 4d.; and
for roasting a buck, given by the mother of
the Lord the King, 2s.; and three pike fish
given to the same lady, 12s. In reward,
given to one of the servants of the same
lady, for carrying the buck to the Mayor and
burgesses, 20d."

On the 29th of November the same year
the Queen gave birth to a daughter, the
Countess being present; and on the following day, which was the Feast of St. Andrew,
the young Princess was baptised in Westminster Abbey. She received the name of
Margaret, in compliment to her grandmother,
who was also her godmother, and whose
present consisted of "a chest of silver and
gilt full of gold."

The Christmas of 1489 again finds the
Countess of Richmond and her husband with
the King and Queen at Westminster. On
New Year's Day they each gave the officers
of arms 20s. During Christmas the Royal
party were entertained with "an Abbot of
misrule that made much sport and did right
well his office." On Candlemas Day the
Countess, with the King and Queen, the

Ambassadors of France, Castille, and the greater part of the lords spiritual and temporal, went in procession to Westminster Hall, where High Mass *in pontificalibus* was said by Richard Fox, Bishop of Winchester, who was also Lord Privy Seal, the Countess' taper being borne by Sir Richard Knevet. In the evening she accompanied the King and Queen to Whitehall, and there "they had a play and a voyde." This last was a light repast or collation of ipocras or other sweet wines, and comfits or sweetmeats, of which the Lady Margaret would partake sparingly ; for Bishop Fisher, in his panegyric, lays stress on her "sober temperance in meat and drink, wherein she lay in as great wait of herself as any person might, keeping always her straight measure, and offending as little as any creature might ; eschewing banquets, rere-soupers, joucrys, and the like." Some eschewing may have been desirable at a time when banquets were wont to last many hours ; it is recorded, as a special mark of abstemiousness of the saintly Bishop himself, that he seldom sat more than an hour at any meal ! And yet in the Countess of Richmond's piety all accounts agree that there was nothing gloomy nor ungracious ;

she was ever ready to rejoice with others and in due season.

In the eighth year of her son's reign the King's mother, by her son's command, prepared a series of "ordinances and reformations of apparel for princes and estates, with other ladies and gentlewomen, for the time of mourning." A mysterious article of dress called a "beke," that had hitherto been used, was prohibited, "on account of its deformity," and a tippet ordered to be worn instead. Ladies not under the degree of a baroness ·were permitted to wear a barb above the chin ; all others, as knight's wives, were directed to wear it under the throat, and other gentlewomen beneath the "throat goyll." Other regulations specify very precisely the size, shape, material, and ornaments of the hoods, trains, surcoats, tippets, mantles, etc., of the various ranks of gentlewomen, forming altogether a curious picture of the funeral costume of the period.

There are not many sources from which to gather information as to the Lady Margaret's lighter tastes or pursuits. Like most of the grandees of the time, she kept a band of minstrels. The Treasurer of Cambridge makes an entry of 10d. paid out for "red wine given to the minstrels of the lady, the King's mother," and one of her singers, Sir John Bracy, was borrowed for a time from her by King Henry; but there is no indication of her having herself played on any musical instrument, as did her daughter-in-law, Queen Elizabeth, who sometimes gave very large sums for her clavicords or lutes. " Dwarfs and jesters she had none; and Henry VII.'s love of menageries and domesticated animals—his pet monkey was almost a historic personage—was evidently not inherited from his mother. Only in goldsmith's work, perhaps the most artistic product of the time, does she seem to have indulged her tastes.

Already in the fourteenth century an immense advance had been made in the preparation of those beautiful translucent enamels, in which the metal was chased and modelled in low relief, and transparent colours laid on, so that when the light passed through them they equalled precious stones in brilliancy. What were called "jewels" in those days, and intended for personal wear, were usually exquisite bits of gold-smith's and enamel work; precious stones were added only to heighten the artistic effect and variety. Ladies' ornaments composed entirely of stones mounted in geometrical or conventional designs, and valued chiefly according to the cost of the materials employed, belong to a later and less artistic age.

Various entries show that Lady Margaret gave away during her lifetime and bequeathed in her will an immense quantity of goldsmith's work—the valuation by probate amounted to £13,000 for the greater plate and jewels, and £2,000 for minor items, which would represent much over £100,000 at the present day. By far the greater portion of this is for church purposes ; still the amount of household plate and jewellery is very large, and in both cases there is constant reference to margarettas (daisies), roses, and the Beaufort portcullis, in the ornamentation, which shows that the articles were made specially to her order. To the Queen and princesses she bequeathed girdles of varying lengths of links, with pomanders or curious knots at the ends ; to them and to other friends rich salt-cellars of gold, garnished with pearls and sapphires ; cups of gold, with covers, some mentioned as "my best gold cups," other six bowls were gold, with red lions graven, one ship of gold, with a little lion on every end of the ship ; to the Lady Mary of Castille, "a standing cup of gold, covered, garnished with white hertes, perles, and stones," weighing thirty-five ounces ; while of plate for church use, crucifixes, chalices, patens, statues of saints, great candlesticks, bowls, censers, graven, chiselled, and enamelled, there is no end. And when we remember how high a value the countrymen and contemporaries of Verrochio and of Ghirlandajo set on English goldsmith's work, we realise that if the intrinsic worth of the Lady Margaret's collection of plate would reach £100,000 of our money, the artistic value would be very much higher. For fine and beautiful embroidery and woven materials, the Countess seems likewise to have had a weakness ; there are many entries in the inventory of her household effects of cloths of gold and verdour, arras, " real and counterfeit," sarsnets, spervers, cloth of gold, silk cushions, and clothes of estate ; among them is one of " an Irish mantell," possibly the gift of her Irish cousin, Lord Howth.

Though the Countess of Richmond was evidently the appreciative owner of a large collection of rare and costly possessions, they probably came to her, for the most part, as incidences of her rank and wealth ; and some portion of them, at least, by inheritance.*

* In Campbell's " Materials for the History of Henry VII." a letter is quoted, addressed by the King to Sir Robert Brackenbury, commanding him to yield up sundry pieces of gold and silver plate " which rightfully belong to our dear and best beloved lady and mother," and restore them to her.

But her more personal and persistent in-
clination, certainly that to which she most
gladly devoted her leisure and her benefactions, was the encouragement of literature,
exhibiting in this the instinct of the time.

For in the last twenty years of the fifteenth century, the country's gain and progress in the "New Learning" had been
immense. Though in 1483 England was
already one of the book marts of the world,
she could not then show a single Greek
scholar ; ten years later saw Grocyn lec-
turing to enthusiastic audiences at Oxford,
where Linacre, who had studied under
Chalcondylas and Polizian, was now a
tutor and had among his pupils young
Thomas More ; even professed ecclesiastics
and zealous parish priests like Colet were
giving up active life for the new studies.
Never has there been a time when the
thoughts and energies of Englishmen were
so concentrated on literature and things of
the intellect: these eager spirits knew nothing
of the desponding pessimism now thought
to belong to a "*fin de siècle*"; they scaled the
upward path of progress with the joyous
alacrity that becomes those on whose fore-
heads the dawning light of a new century is
already reflected.

A poet of modern times, wishing to express his exultation when a faithful and adequate translation first revealed to him the unsuspected grandeur of Homer, compared it with that of

> . . . stout Cortez when with eagle eyes
> He stared at the Pacific—and all his men
> Looked at each other with a wild surmise,
> Silent—upon a peak of Darien.

But to an Englishman of Henry VII.'s time Keats' famous simile would have seemed wholly inadequate, for we are told that in those days " Picus Mirandula was more thought of than Cabot or Vespucci ; one who had come from Italy than one who had discovered Newfoundland." Not that transalpine visitors were rare or passing apparitions ; the prodigality of a rich and generous nation had already provided such endowments that students were coming in from all tribes and peoples to what seemed the fountain-head of scholarship. In 1499 Erasmus had written : " I have found in Oxford so much polish and learning that I now scarcely care to go to Italy, save for the sake of saying I have been there."

The era was not, however, one of much literary production ; the continual fresh discoveries of ancient manuscripts, a rapid progress in philology, deeper insight into the mysteries of language, and closer acquaintance with classic ideals sufficed even the most fervid enthusiasts. As Ruskin has put it : "We imitate, but do not reverence our forefathers ; the mediævals reverenced, but did not strive to imitate the classics." Instead of wishing to stamp their new found treasures with their own image and superscription, they were eager rather to pass them on from hand to hand ; and in this work of the spreading and distribution of knowledge the Countess of Richmond took an active part : her name is frequently and gratefully mentioned by the writers and publishers of her own and the succeeding generation. Wynkyn de Worde styled himself " Printer to the King's mother"; Pynson she also helped and patronised ; and her acts of kindness to men of letters, students, and the poor scholars for whom the enlightened charity of the period did so much, were innumerable. However, the first instance of the Countess of Richmond's exercise of literary patronage is a very modest one ; in 1489 Caxton printed the " History of Kynge Blanchandyne and Queen Eglantyne," of which he says in the preface that he had received the book from the redoubtable lady the Duchess of Somerset, the King's mother, to whom not long before he had sold it, knowing it to be honest and joyful, and now at her command had translated it into our maternal tongue. Caxton goes on to ask pardon for the rude and common English, which he hopes, however, will be " understanded of readers and hearers. And that shall suffice."*

A little later, after Caxton's death, his successor, Wynkyn de Worde, printed in folio a book written by Walter Hylton, entitled " The Scale of Perfection," at the command of the Countess of Richmond. This treatise on the spiritual life, written by an obscure author in a small house of the Augustinian Canons in the North of England, had a remarkable fate. Addressed to the Carthusian, that most solitary of all the varieties of the monastic life, it became the guide to generations of good Christians, both at Court and in the world. Through the dismal Wars of the Roses, and afterwards through the terrible ordeal of the Tudor persecutions, many a heart was strengthened

* It is curious that Caxton should address his patroness as Duchess of Somerset, a title to which she could never have had any claim. Even if the Dukedom of Somerset had been transmissible to females in default of the male line, it would have been inherited by the daughters of Edmund, second Duke of Somerset, who fell at St. Albans, 1455.

and comforted by Walter Hylton. The very copy still exists which must have been in the hands of the martyred Carthusians,* the glow from whose pallid faces lit up the cell of Sir Thomas More as he watched them on their way to execution ; and though the number of its English readers grew gradually fewer as the Catholic ranks thinned, yet there are editions dated 1659 and 1679.

Fuller, in his "Church History," mentions a book of prayers "printed by the commandement of the most high and virtuous Princess our liege lady Elizabeth, Queen of England, and of the most noble Princess Margaret, mother of our Lord the King"; from the way in which Fuller alludes to this book, he seems himself to have seen it, but no other notice of the volume can be traced.

About 1507 Richard Pynson published a book entitled "The Mirror of Gold for the Sinful Soul," copies of which still exist, that are reckoned among the most beautiful specimens of English typography. It had been originally written in Latin under the name of "Speculum Aureum peccatorum"; from the Latin it was translated into French, and after this translation had been seen

---

* "Essay on the Spiritual Life of Mediæval England,'' p. 36. Rev. J. B. Dalgairns, Oratorian.

and corrected by many clerks (clerics),
doctors, and masters in divinity, it was
again translated by the Countess of
Richmond herself from French into English. This exceedingly rare book, which
is described at some length in Cooper's
volume, is said by him to contain fifty-
four leaves decorated with borders running
round every page, "in imitation of the illu-
minated MSS. of the previous age." It was
first printed without date by Richard Pynson, London, in quarto, and divided into
seven chapters, after the seven days of the
week. This arrangement, the preface intimates, is to the intent that the soul may in
every chapter have a new mirror wherein
to behold and consider herself. The work
is embellished with woodcuts of the Prophet
Jeremiah, of St. Matthew, and St. John;
another represents a sort of portico in which
Death strikes at a man with a dart. At the beginning of the seventh chapter is a woodcut
representing the Son of Man sitting with
uplifted hands; on His right are two angels,
one of whom is raising the dead by the sound
of a trumpet ; and on His left likewise two
angels, one playing on a violin; at his feet four
angels are gathering together the elect and
carrying them to Heaven in a sheet. Cooper

goes on to say that the book had considerable popularity in its day, having been reprinted in 1522 both by Wynkyn de Worde and John Skot, and again by the former in 1526.

Dyce, in his notice of Shelton, alludes to the Countess of Richmond as being well known to have used her utmost exertions for the advancement of literature ; adding that she herself translated some pieces from the French, and that under her patronage several works were rendered into English by the most competent scholars of the time. Dyce thinks it is to her that Shelton alludes in a passage of "Garlande of Lawrell," in which he mentions one of his lost performances.

The "Nicodemus Gospel" seems to have been printed by Wynkyn de Worde at the Countess' desire, also the prose translation of "The greate Shyppe of Fooles," in the preface to which (though it was not printed till 1517) Henry Watson states that he "translated it to our maternal tongue of English, through the exhortation of the excellent Princess Margaret, Countess of Richmond, grandame to our Sovereign Lord King Henry VIII."

In 1503 Wynkyn de Worde, by the Countess of Richmond's direction, brought out the first edition printed in English* of the "Imi-

* Of an earlier English translation of the "Imitatio," two

tation of Christ." Of this very rare book the British Museum has a single and beautifully printed copy. The elaborately designed title-page is framed by little compartments, each containing an emblem of the Passion ; it has a woodcut of " Our Lady of Pity," and the Countess' own monogram, the letter M enclosing the portcullis of the Beauforts. An introductory paragraph says that the book was translated from the Latin of Master John Gerson, Chancellor of the University of Paris, by Dr. William Atkynson, Doctor of Divinity. This, however, only applies to the first three books of the "Imitation "; the fourth book, treating of the Sacrament of the Altar, though bound up in one volume with the others, has its own title-page, telling that it was translated from the French of Gerson by the Countess herself, " in the form and manner ensuing."

Dr. Ingram, now Vice-Provost of Trinity College, Dublin, who has edited a reprint

MSS. copies exist ; one is at Cambridge, the other in the library of Trinity College, Dublin. Dr. Ingram, who edited a reprint of the Trinity College MSS. for the Early English Text Society, says that these two translations are identical, and date from about 1460 (though the Cambridge copy is catalogued as dating from 1400). Several trifling errors occur in both copies, in both the quotation from Ovid, " Nihil obstat," Book I., chap. iii., is omitted ; while Book IV. of the " Imitation " is not included in either the Cambridge or in the Dublin MSS. (See Note in Appendix.)

of the Countess of Richmond's translation of the "Imitatio" for the Early English Text Society, thinks that she used the first French translation, which was published at Toulouse in 1488. He points out a few errors in her text, of which the most noteworthy are the following: "advertence" for "inadvertence"; "ineffabilis" translated instead of "infallibilis"; "innocent" for "incontinent"; "ye" for "he"; "effectual" as rendering for "affectuosa"; "holiest" apparently for "holifest"; and "open" as rendering "operari," probably by a confusion of the French "ouvrer" with "ouvrir." On the other hand, her translation of the third verse of the fourteenth chapter of Book IV., which hardly any two other English translators render alike, is the most accurate: she gives "proveable" for "probabile," which the other translators either render as "probable," or by some circumlocution arrive at the obvious meaning of the verse. Indeed, this lady has kept so closely to the text of the original version as to suggest that her knowledge of Latin must have been very inadequately described as "a little perceiving." And throughout, her work is distinctly superior in style to that of Atkynson, and singularly free from what

145

L

Campbell, in his "Essay on English Poetry," calls "the prevailing fault of English diction in the fifteenth century, the affectation of Anglicising Latin words . . . the writers of that period tore up words from the Latin, which never took root in the language, like children making a mock garden with flowers and branches stuck in the ground, which speedily wither."

The following reprint of the third chapter of the Lady Margaret's translation, in which the spelling has been modernised, but the language left as it stands in the original, differs less from modern English than that of many later writers, and can, I think, be read with pleasure even now :

"Lord, I come unto Thee, to the end that health may come unto me of Thy gift, and that I may joy at the holy feast that Thou hast made ready unto me, by Thy sweet benignity, in the which my Saviour is all that I may or ought to desire ; for Thou art my health, my redemption, my strength, honour, and joy. Alas! my Lord God, make the soul of Thy daily servant joyous, for my Lord Jesus, I have raised my soul unto Thee, and now desire devoutly and reverently to receive Thee into my house, to the end that I may deserve with Zacheus to be blessed of Thee, and to be accounted among the children of Abraham. My soul desireth Thy body, my heart desireth to be united and onely with Thee ; give Thyself unto me, good Lord, and then I suffice, for without Thee no consolation nor comfort is good ; without Thee I may not be, and without Thy visitation I may not live. Wherefore it behoveth me oftentimes to come and approach Thy high presence, to receive Thee for the remedy of my health, to the intent I fall not in the way of this mortal life, if I were defrauded from Thy spiritual nourishing.

"Also, my right merciful Lord Jesu, when Thou has preached unto the people and healed them of divers sickness, Thou hast said : 'I will not leave them fasting, and without any refection, lest peradventure they might fall in their way.' Do with me then, good Lord, in that manner, sythen Thou has left this holy sacrament for the comfort of all faithful people ; for Thou art the sweet refection of the souls of them that have worthily received and eaten Thee, and they shall be partners and inheritors of the eternal joy. Certain it is unto me necessary, that so often sin, and so soon cool (am lukewarm), and at every hour fail to come unto the end, that by continual orisons and confessions, and by the receiving of Thy holy body I may purify and renew the heat of my refection. For, peradventure, in abstaining me too long to receive Thee, I may leave, forget, and run from my holy purpose. For the wit of man and woman, from their childhood, be inclined unto all evil. And also if this divine and godly medicine help us not, innocent (incontinently or quickly) we fall to worse. Then this holy communion draweth men from evil, and comforteth them again in goodness. For I am many times very negligent, and very often cold when I commune with or worship my God; what then should I do if I took not that medicine, and asked not grace and help of Him? And albeit I am not always well-disposed to receive my Creator, yet shall I put me in pain to receive these sacred mysteries in time conveniable (convenient), so that I may be made a partner of so great a grace. For it is one of the most principal and greatest consolations unto faithful souls for the time they shall make their pilgrimage in this mortal body, and to the end we may have more mind of Thy benefits. My Lord God, I shall more often receive Thee, my loving Lord, with a devout thought. O marvellous gentleness! Of Thine unspeakable pity towards us, that Thou, Lord God,

Creator and Giver of life unto all spirits, hast willed to come to so poor a soul with the Deity and Humanity, and my poor lean and hungry soul hath listed to be made fat with Thy grace and the holy unction of Thy sweet spirit. O happy thought and well-happy soul, that deserveth devoutly to receive his God, his Lord and Creator, and in that receiving to be filled with joy and spiritual gladness. O what great Lord receivest thou? O what and how great a host entertainest thou in Thy lodging? How joyous a companion takest Thou into Thy house? How faithful a friend Thou admittest unto Thee? How good, noble, and sweet a spouse embracest Thou? which ought to be beloved and desired above all things. O right, sweet beloved Lord, the heavens and the earth and all the ornaments of them hold silence in the presence of Thy face. For what praising, honour, and beauty they have, it is of Thy mercy and largeness, and cannot be like unto the beauty and honour of Thy holy name, of Thy sapience, whereof there is neither number nor end."

In giving to her country people the first English edition of the "Imitatio," the Countess of Richmond assuredly, though unwittingly, was acting in her distinctive character of peace-bringer. For within twenty years after her death began the long period during which everything that recalled the ancient faith of the land was contemned—the whole religious literature of mediæval England practically stamped out. But while the words of Holy Writ, the great patristic authors, the histories of the Saints, the very fabrics of the churches became occasions of strife and contention, the " Imitatio " alone wrought no ministry but that of healing, brought no message save that of peace. How many harsh judgments must have been softened? how many bitter prejudices overcome? when those who had been taught to look on the Catholic Church as Babylon, on her religious orders as the body-guard of Satan, found in the words of a tonsured monk, written in " the most benighted period of the Dark Ages," the most adequate expression of their spiritual needs and yearnings, the surest guidance for their inner lives, given with a simplicity and authority, the secret of which succeeding generations had lost.

And even in our own days, when a contest, less violent in its methods, but infinitely more terrible in its issues, is being fought out—not between the champions of conflicting creeds, but between faith and unbelief, between the spirit of negation and the spirit of Christ, the small thin volume, "which you may buy for a sixpence at a bookstall," is, from its very humility, so lifted up that all men's hearts are drawn to it. The philosophic altruist apologises for his well-worn copy by telling you that it contains the best exposition he knows of the law of self-sacrifice ; the Comtist, like his master, reads his daily chapter, holding that they who do not accept its theological tenets may use it for the purpose of moral self-culture. But never, perhaps, do we see more plainly how strong has been its silent influence on natures which seem the least prepared to receive it, than in the strikingly beautiful passage where one who often saw George Eliot in her last days notes, "The 'Imitatio' was never far from her hand." And by the generation for whose benefit the Lady Margaret's translation was made it was instantly appreciated ; before the year was out Pynson brought out a second edition, and others followed quickly. Pynson also printed a revised and corrected edition of the breviary, *secundum usum Sarum*, at the expense of the Countess, but at what time does not appear.

From King Henry's Privy Purse expenses

we learn that on the 2nd October, 1493, he was his mother's guest at Colyweston, where he seems to have remained some little time, for on the 16th is a charge for "carrying the King's harness from Colyweston to Stony Stratford"; and on the 18th February following the same book contains an entry of ten shillings paid to the Countess' minstrels.

On the eve of St. Simon and St. Jude, 1494, the Lady Margaret accompanied the King and Queen from Sheen to Westminster, and was present at the solemn installation of her favourite grandchild, Prince Henry, as Duke of York, which took place at the ensuing Feast of ALL HALLOWS, on which occasion she is described as following the Queen, wearing a coronet. She was also present at the joustings, which were afterwards held in honour of the Prince's creation, and in compliment to her god-daughter, Princess Margaret.

These festivities were the last in which, for a lengthened period, the Countess of Richmond took part, for the quiet tenour of her life was rudely broken by the shock of a great tragedy which plunged the house of Stanley into the deepest mourning.

Three years before, in the spring of 1492, Perkin Warbeck landed from the Low

Countries in Cork, and gave himself out to be the Duke of York. He was acknowledged both in Ireland and by James III. of Scotland; on his return to Flanders the Duchess Dowager of Burgundy, the sister of Edward IV., who was generally believed to have caused Warbeck to be trained for his part, openly received him as her nephew. For a time Henry VII. seems not to have troubled himself as to this fresh impostor; but when Charles VIII. of France and Maximilian of Germany affected to recognise Warbeck's claim, and gave him promises of support, above all, when the Duchess succeeded in gaining over the King's own private secretary, Frion, and through his help and counsel began to make her Court a rallying-point for all disaffected English subjects, he acted promptly and with vigour, causing Lord Fitzwalter, with several others, to be arrested and tried. All were convicted of treason, and the three principal conspirators immediately executed. Some weeks later a formal court of inquiry was held in the Tower, and then, to the consternation of all, the Lord High Chamberlain, Sir William Stanley, was impeached on the evidence of Sir Robert Clifford. The King, Lord Bacon writes, seemed as much amazed at the naming of this lord as if he had seen some fearful prodigy. To hear that a man who had done him services of such a nature as to save his life and to set his crown on his head ; one so near him in alliance—his brother having married the King's mother— one to whom, as making him Chamberlain, he had committed the care of his person, should be thus false to him, was a staggering blow. Clifford was requested over and over again to repeat the particulars of his accusation, and warned that in a matter so unlikely he should not go too far. But as he repeated his first statement steadily and constantly, the King desired Sir William Stanley to be restrained to his own chamber. On the day following, when he was arraigned before the Lords for high treason, "his pleading was very slender, denying little he was charged with, thereby, as it were, pleading guilty, so that he was adjudged to die."

Had the King been out of fear for his own estate, he would, Lord Bacon thinks, have pardoned Stanley ; and all writers agree that the conflict in Henry's mind was most acute. "But the cloud of so great a rebellion hanging over his head, made him work sure," and after an interval of six weeks, honourably interposed, Stanley was executed on the 16th of February, 1495. Although it has been said—and probably in reference to the same matter—"that although Henry loved and revered his mother, yet he was in no wise led by her," it is surprising that no evidence exists of the Lady Margaret having interceded for her brother-in-law, especially as the blow was very deeply felt by both her and her husband. It is expressly stated that the Earl of Derby and his Countess after these untoward events quitted the Court and went down to Lathom, where they remained for many months in strict seclusion and mourning, as if overwhelmed with grief at the death of so dear and valued a relative.* The most probable explanation is that Stanley's guilt was greater than had been deemed prudent to disclose, and that the good of the country made it imperative that the nearness to the King's person in office and in alliance, which made his treachery greater,

* It was rumoured that the chief accusation brought against Stanley was, that he had said "that he would never bear arms against Warbeck, if he were sure that he were King Edward's son." But it can hardly be imagined that an accusation founded on mere words would have induced the King to forget Stanley's services, and disregard his close connection with Lord Derby and with his own mother. The result of the trial rather confirms the assertion made in many old chronicles, that Stanley had for some time been abetting Warbeck, and had advanced him considerable sums of money (Halsted).

should not be the cause of his escaping with impunity, when others less deeply implicated paid the forfeit of their lives.

That Henry was not forgetful of Stanley's past services is shown by his paying his debts and giving him an honourable burial at Lyon and at his own charge. Nor does the tragic occurrence seem to have left any bitterness behind, for a few months later the King and Queen went in progress " to comfort his mother, whom ¡he also did love and revere, and to make demonstration that the proceedings imposed upon him by necessity of state had not in the least diminished the affection he bore to the noble Earl, his father-in-law." Lord Derby, apprised of the honour intended, and of the King's wish to commiserate and condole with him and with his mother in their affliction, made suitable preparation for receiving him with due respect and honour. With all haste possible he beautified his seats of Lathom and Knowsley, considerably enlarging the latter, for the better accommodation of the King and Queen with their respective suites, as they were to rest there for some days before proceeding to Lathom. There being at that time no certain or continued passage over the river Mersey, he built a bridge and threw up a

causeway across the marshes to the rising
ground on the Cheshire side, that the Royal
party might pursue their progress without
delay or hazard.

After he had started, the King received
intelligence that Perkin Warbeck was hover-
ing with a fleet on the coast of Kent, and
therefore proposed to break off his journey
and return to London ; but on the following
morning, being apprised that Perkin had
abandoned his intention of landing, he and
the Queen travelled on to Lathom, which
was reached on the 30th of June. On the
3rd of July they were at Knowsley, and
from the 4th to the 11th of September
King Henry seems to have stayed on
alone at his mother's house at Colyweston.
The various stages of this lengthened progress may be seen in the King's Privy
Purse expenses. That Queen Elisabeth
accompanied her husband is shown by
an entry, made at Lathom, of a charge
of 6s. 8d. " To the women that sung before the King and the Queen in rewarde."

CHAPTER VII.

IT is sometimes given as a reason why the history of the fifteenth century in England has aroused so little interest, that the period is exceptionally poor in historic authorities, and that very few private letters have been preserved; it may partly, the Bishop of Oxford thinks, have been owing to the recent substitution of paper for parchment : a new material so intrinsically worthless, and yet so useful for lighting fires, was likely to prove a temptation to destruction not easily resisted. Moreover, times were dangerous, people wrote sparingly, and only what it was safe to write, so that it is not surprising that from the Countess of Richmond's correspondence but few letters have survived : these mostly belong to the last decade of her life, and relate to a claim on the King of France for money advanced by her mother, the late Duchess of Somerset, to his great-uncle, John of Orleans, who was for many years a prisoner in England, and lived in the quaint and beautiful old mansion of Groombridge Place, in Kent, one of the few pre-Tudor houses still inhabited and in admirable preservation.

The first of these letters is to her son, and is dated "Colyweston, 14th January." From the reference to a Cardinal, who certainly was Morton, Mr. Cooper says it must have been written in or before the year 1500.

"My own sweet and most dear King, and all my worldly joy.

"In as humble manner as I can think, I recommend me to your Grace, and most heartily beseech Our Lord to bless you. And, my good heart, where that you say that the French King hath at this time given me courteous answer, and written letters of favour to his court of Parliament for the brief expedition of my matter, which so long hath hanged ; the which I well know he doth especially for your sake, for the which my . . . ly beseech your Grace it . . . to give him your favourable thanks, and to desire him to continue his . . . in . . . e . . . me. And, if it so might like your Grace, to do the same to the Cardinal, which, as I understood, is your faithful, true, and loving servant. I wish, my very joy, as I oft have showed,

and I fortune to get this, or any part
thereof, there shall neither be that or any
good I have, but it shall be yours, and at
your commandment, as surely and with as
good a will as any ye have in your coffers;
and would God ye could know it, as verily
as I think it. But, my dear heart, I will no
more encumber your Grace with further
writing in this matter, for I am sure your
chaplain and servant, Dr. Whytston, hath
showed your Highness the circumstances
of the same; and, if it so may please your
Grace, I humbly beseech the same, to give
further credence also to this bearer. And
Our Lord give you as long good life, health,
and joy, as your most noble heart can desire,
with as hearty blessing as Our Lord hath
given me power to give you.

"At Colyweston, the 14th day of January,
by your faithful, true bedewoman and humble
mother,
"MARGARET R."

It is evident, from the date of the following letter, that the Countess of Richmond
wrote from Calais; but her reason for going
there is not known. From the allusion to
the election of the Bishop of Ely (her stepson, Stanley) it was probably written in 1501.
The conclusion shows that her son, King

Henry VII., was born on the 26th of July, and is the only authority for that fact.

" My dearest, and only desired joy in this world,

"With my most hearty loving blessings, and humble commendations, I pray Our Lord to reward and thank your Grace, for that it hath pleased your Highness so kindly and lovingly to be content to write your letters of thanks to the French King for my great matter that so long hath been in suit, as Master Welby hath showed me your bounteous goodness is pleased. I wish, my dear heart, and my fortune be to recover it, I trust ye shall well perceive I shall deal towards you as a kind, loving mother ; and if I should never have it, yet your kind dealing is to me a thousand times more than all that gold I can recover, and all the French King's might be mine withal. My dear heart, and it may please your Highness to license Master Whitstongs for this time to present your honourable letters, and begin the process of my cause ; for that he so well knoweth the matter, and also brought me the writings from the said French King, with his other letters to his Parliament at Paris, it should be greatly to my help, as I

161

M

think ; but all will I remit to your pleasure ;
and if I be too bold in this, or any of my
desires, I humble beseech your grace of
pardon, and that your Highness take no
displeasure.

"My good King, I have now sent a servant of mine into Kendall, to receive such
annuities as be yet hanging upon the account
of Sir William Wall, my Lord's chaplain,
whom I have clearly discharged ; and if it
will please your Majesty's own heart, at your
leisure, to send me a letter and command
me that I suffer none of my tenants be retained with no man, but that they be kept
for my Lord of York,* your fair sweet son,
for whom they be most meet, it shall be a
good excuse for me to my lord and husband ; and then I may well,. and without
displeasure, cause them all to be sworn, the
which shall not after be long undone. And
where your Grace showed your pleasure for
. . . the bastard of King Edward's ;
there is neither that or any other thing I
may do by your commandment, but I shall
be glad to fulfil to my little power, with
God's grace. And, my sweet King, Field-
ing, this bearer, hath prayed me to beseech
you to be his good lord in a matter he sueth

* Afterwards King Henry VIII.

for to the Bishop of Ely (now, as we hear, elect) for a little office nigh to London. Verily, my King, he is a good and a wise well-ruled gentleman, and full truly hath served you, well accompanied, as well at your first as all other occasions; and that causeth us to be the more bold and gladder also to speak for him; howbeit, my Lord Marquis hath been very low to him in times past, because he would not be retained with him; and truly, my good King, he helped me right well in such matters as I have business within these parts. And, my dear heart, I now beseech you of pardon of my long and tedious writing, and pray Almighty God to give you as long, good, and prosperous life as ever had Prince; and as hearty blessings as I can ask of God.

"At Calais town, this day of St. Anne's, that I did bring into this world my good and gracious Prince, King, and only beloved son, by

"Your humble servant, bedewoman,

and Mother,

"MARGARET R."

The annexed letter from King Henry VII., though in one portion it evidently refers to business of the French debt, yet we see

from the mention of Fisher and of the Westminster and Cambridge foundations that it
must have been written at a good deal later
date than the previous from one his mother.

" Madam, my most entirely well - beloved
lady and mother,

" I recommend me unto you in the most
humble and lowly wise that I can, beseeching you of your daily and continual blessings. By your confessor, the bearer, I have
received your good and most loving writing,
and by the same have heard at good leisure
such credence as he would show unto me on
your behalf, and thereupon have sped him
in every behalf without delay, according to
your noble petition and desire which resteth
in two principal points ; the one for a general
pardon of all manner of causes ; the other is
for to alter and change part of a licence
which I have given unto you before, for to
be put into mortmain at Westminster and
now to be converted into the University of
Cambridge for your soul's health, etc. All
which things according to your desire and
pleasure, I have with all my heart and goodwill given and granted unto you. And my
Dame, not only in this, but in all other
things that I may know should be to your

honour and pleasure, and weal of your soul, I shall be as glad to please you as your heart can desire it ; and I know well that I am as much bounden so to do as any creature living, for the great and singular motherly love and affection that it hath pleased you at all times to bear towards me. Wherefore, my own most loving Mother, in my most hearty manner I thank you, beseeching you of your good continuance in the same. And Madam, your said confessor hath moreover shown unto me on your behalf, that ye, of your goodness and kind disposition, have given and granted unto me such title and interest as ye have or ought to have in such debts and duties which is owing and due unto you in France, by the French King and others ; wherefore, Madam, in my most hearty and humble wise, I thank you. Howbeit, I verily think it will be right hard to recover it without it be driven by compulsion and force, rather than by any true justice, which is not yet as we think any convenient time to be put in execution.

" Nevertheless, it hath pleased you to give us a good interest and mean, if they will not conform them to reason and good justice, to defend or offend at a convenient time when the case shall so require hereafter. For such a chance may fall that this your grant might stand in great stead for a recovery of our right, and to make us free, whereas we be now bound, etc. And verily, Madam, and I might recover it at this time or any other, ye be sure ye should have your pleasure therein, as I and all that God has given me, is and shall ever be at your will and commandment, as I have instructed Master Fisher more largely herein, as I doubt not but he will declare unto you. And I beseech you to send me your mind and pleasure in the same, which I shall be full glad to follow with God's grace, which send and give unto you the full accomplishment of all your noble and virtuous desires.

" Written at Greenwich, 17th day of July, with the hand of your most · humble and loving son,

" H. R.

" After the writing of this letter your confessor delivered unto me such letters and writings obligatory of your duties in France, which it hath pleased you to send unto me, which I have received by an indenture of every parcel of the same. Wherefore, eftsoons, in my most humble wise, I thank you, and I purpose hereafter, at better leisure, to know your mind and pleasure further therein. Madam, I have encumbered you now with this my long writings, but methinks that I can do no less, considering it is so seldom I do write ; wherefore I beseech you to pardon me, for verily, Madam, my sight is nothing so perfect as it has been, and I know well it will impair daily, wherefore I trust that you will not be displeased though I write not so often with my own hand, for, on my faith, I have been three days or I could make an end of this letter.

" To my Lady."

The allusion in King Henry's letter to his failing sight has a certain pathos, from being addressed by a man who has not yet reached his fiftieth year, to his mother still in full health and vigour, and who seems almost to the last to have kept all her faculties exercised and unimpaired, while he aged prematurely. Only sixteen years had elapsed since his soldiers' shout had hailed him the victor of Bosworth, and the people as they saw him pass cried out " God bless that fair-favoured face ! " And though the time that intervened had been full of strifes and struggles, yet he had come well through of them : unlike the warriors of ancient Gaul, of whom it used to be said, " They go out bravely to battle, but they always fall," it was noted of Henry that " whenever he went out to battle, he came back the victor." His chronicler, Bernard Andreas, in fanciful and far-fetched allegory (worked out, however, with clearness and minuteness), compares him to the Hercules of the twelve labours; as having overcome the Nemean lion in Edward IV.; the Eryman-thian boar in Richard III.; the Arcadian stag in John of Lincoln ; the Cretan bull in James of Scotland ; the mares of Diomedes in Martin Swart ; whose hydra had been the civil wars ; who had put down the Stym-phalian birds by the agency of the Star Chamber ; had thwarted in Margaret of York the host of the Amazons ; and found the three heads of Geryon in Maximilian, the Archduke Philip and the Dowager of Bur-gundy : who had beaten Cacus in Perkin Warbeck and Cerberus in three more insig-nificant enemies, and by overcoming Maxi-milian's opposition to the French alliance had lulled the dragon and made his way to the Garden of the Hesperides!

But Henry was not a warlike or turbulent nature to whom the fruits of war would have been sweet, but rather a sensitive and peace-loving man, given to be troubled by

the feeling of insecurity which dogged his
triumphs, and often deeply pained by the
slight grounds on which those much indebted to him renounced their allegiance :
as was the case when his mother-in-law
intrigued against him, and John de la
Pole took up arms—neither of them having anything to gain by his loss, but
seemingly joining his enemies only to create
confusion. Then, the infliction of punishment, which was one of the necessities
of victory, was always distasteful to him ; for,
as Bacon allows, " with his justice, he was a
merciful Prince," "never was so great rebellion expiated with so little blood as those of
Blackheath and Exeter"; and his conduct in
sparing the lives of rebels taken red-handed
as were Lambert Simnel and Perkin Warbeck, was quite without example in his day.
We have seen how the execution of Stanley
affected him, and it was said that he only
consented to that of Warwick (which certainly is the greatest blot on his reputation)
on what seemed but a doubtfully proved
treason, with deep repugnance. Puebla, the
Spanish Envoy, wrote home, that when he
saw the King a fortnight later he seemed to
have aged by twenty years. But the most
sympathetic and perfect estimate of Henry

VII.'s character and qualities is that of Mrs. J. R. Green.

" In the delicate, careworn face, with its suggestion of undeviating self-effacement ; in the penetrating intelligence, devoted to the apprehending of the new problems and the infinite labour spent in solving them ; in the inscrutable acquiescence with which 'loving to seal up his own dangers' he carried the burdens that were henceforth to fall to the lot of kings, and in the unflinching resolution of his methods, we recognise a new type of Royal dignity."

Early in 1502, on the promotion of her chaplain and confessor, Dr. Richard Fitzjames, to the See of Rochester, the King's mother appointed in his stead Dr. John Fisher, who had so large a share in the collegiate foundations and other good works which filled the last years of her life that a slight sketch of his history and character will not be out of place.   The son of a well-to-do burgess of Beverley—a town which, owing to its great scholastic formations and establishments, was of much greater importance then than now—Fisher, who lost his father early in life, went in 1483 as a student to Cambridge.   According to one tradition he entered the College of God's House, which he was afterwards instrumental in rebuilding under

the name of Christ's. But his latest biographer, Father Bridgett, questions this, on
the ground that in his early years Fisher was
certainly under the care of William de Melton,
a fellow of Michael's House. In 1492 he
was himself elected Fellow of this College,
and in 1494, while he was Senior Proctor, the
business of the University took him to the
Court, which was then at Greenwich. And
the Proctor's book containing the entry of
the expenses of this journey has this note
written by Fisher in Latin : " I dined with
the Lady Mother of the King." The acquaintance thus begun between the young
priest and the noble lady ripened into mutual
esteem and confidence : each possessed the
qualities which the other most highly appreciated. " Never, perhaps," writes Father
Bridgett, "lived there a man in England who
more thoroughly illustrated the heavenly
character of the Christian priesthood as he
himself has described it." The same writer
thinks that the portrait in the dining hall of
St. John's, Cambridge, which is said to represent Fisher, is merely a fancy portrait ;
but that the red chalk drawing by Holbein,
now in the British Museum, with its honest,
modest, but anxious and conscientious expression, shows completely the man whose

wonderful purity of life, combined with profound but unostentatious learning and peculiar kindliness of manner, so deeply impressed Erasmus.

In 1497 Fisher was made Master of Michaelhouse College, and in 1501 he became Vice-Chancellor of the University, and might well have thought, as did another saintly recluse, that the snapdragon, which doubtless even then had made its home in the crannies of the already ancient University walls, would be the fittest emblem of his ' future life ; but other work lay before him. The first-fruits, as regards the University of Cambridge, of Fisher's guidance of the Countess of Richmond, was the endowment of the readerships already mentioned in Cambridge and in Oxford ; another foundation, which followed in 1504, was that of preachers "to the praise and honour of the Holy name of Jesus and the Annunciation of the Blessed Virgin Mary." Six sermons were to be preached annually : one on a Sunday, either at St. Paul's Cross, St. Margaret, Westminster, or some notable church in the City of London ; and one during the same term on some feast-day, in each of the churches of Ware and Cheshunt in Hertfordshire ; Bassingbourne, Orwell, and Babraham, in Cambridgeshire ; Maxey, St. James Deeping, Bowen, Boston, and Gunnishead, in Lincolnshire. The locality and grouping of the churches named makes it evident that the Countess' intention was that the poorest and remotest parishes on her estates should have the best instruction attainable in religious matters ; for the preacher was to be a perpetual Fellow of some College in Cambridge.

As year followed year the Countess of Richmond's time came to be more and more filled up by works of charity and piety, so that her name occurs less frequently at Court festivities in the later than in the earlier period of her son's reign. However, in all family rejoicings and gatherings she still took part, and special mention is made of her being present at the marriage of her grandson, Arthur, Prince of Wales, with Katherine of Aragon. The Spanish Princess should have been a bride after the Countess' own heart, for she was of Lancastrian descent through her great-grandmother, Constantia, daughter of John of Gaunt, and cultured enough to satisfy so severe a critic as Erasmus, who wrote that by the care of her illustrious mother (herself one of the

most learned ladies of her day) Doña
Caterina "was imbued with learning from
her earliest years." She had the advantage (of which the Countess of Richmond
often bewailed her own neglect) of a thorough knowledge of Latin, which language
she could read and write fluently ; but English was not among the studies of even
the most learned ladies of those days, and it
was a matter of some anxiety to Queen Isa-
bella how her daughter would be able to
hold intercourse with her new relatives until
she had mastered it. Fortunately, the
Spanish Ambassador was able to send his
Royal mistress the comforting assurance
that both the Queen of England and the
King's mother spoke French fluently, and
had rejoiced on hearing that Doña Caterina,
whom they were preparing to welcome with
all love and tenderness, was likewise perfect
mistress of that language.

The Princess Katherine reached London
early in November, and was received with a
degree of splendour that gave much satisfac-
tion to the Spaniards, who, according to their
chronicler, Bernaldo, sent home word that
the English fully deserved the reputation
they had always had of "giving to accept-
able and beloved strangers wonderful wel-

comes." The marriage was solemnised with great magnificence at Westminster. Blessed Fisher, in his " Mornynge Remembrance of the Lady Margaret," says that at the great triumph of her grandson's marriage " she wept marvellously, in dread that some adversity might follow," as if intimating that the pious and revered lady had something of the gift of prophecy ; for it was then fresh in the minds of his hearers that the bride at whose wedding she had shed those tears had become within six months time a widow. But Fisher did not foresee that there was still greater cause for sorrow, in that the marriage solemnised with such rejoicing was to be the first link in a long chain of events which was to end in the uprooting of England's ancient faith, and in his own death on the scaffold. However, notwithstanding her forebodings, the Countess of Richmond and her husband played their parts handsomely in the marriage festivities. On the 15th of November she entertained at Coldharbour the principal nobles and gentry of Spain, " for whom the place was right royally and pleasantly beseen and addressed, hung with rich cloth of arras, and in the hall a goodly cupboard made and erected with great plenty both of silver and gold ; and there were set at the board coupled and accompanied every one of them, the men as well as the women, with his and her companion of England, to make them great cheer and solace. They were also served in right good manner with victuals delicate and dainty, and with divers wines abundant and plenteous." When the time of feasting had come to an end, and the greater number of the Spanish ladies who had formed part of Katherine's suite, began to prepare for the homeward journey, the little bride of fifteen grew sad and mournful at parting from the friends of her youth ; King Henry seeing this, took her into his library and showed her many goodly books, both in English and in Latin. Then, when her cheerfulness was somewhat restored, he brought forward a jeweller, with a collection of rings and gauds, bidding her choose from them what she would, and what remained he himself divided among the Spanish ladies she was allowed to keep in her service and her newly - appointed English ladies. A few weeks later the youthful bride and bride-groom went to keep Court at Ludlow Castle ; but before six months had elapsed, when the King and Queen were at Greenwich, a messenger came post-haste from

Ludlow to the Lords of the Privy Council, bringing the tidings of Prince Arthur's death. They decided to send the King's confessor to break the news to him. Accordingly, at a very early hour the next morning the friar entered the Royal chamber, and, desiring that all present might retire, he approached the King, saying, " If we receive good from the Lord's hand shall we not also receive evil, and patiently sustain the ills He sends us?" He then showed the King that his dear son, the Prince of Wales, was departed to God. When the King understood the sorrowful heavy tidings he sent for the Queen, saying that he and his wife would bear their sorrow together.

After she was come, and saw the King, her lord, in that natural and painful sorrow, she, with full and great and constant comfortable words besought him that he would, after God, consider the weal of his own noble person, the realm, and her. " And," added the Queen, " remember that my lady, your mother, never bore children but you only, yet God, by His grace, has ever preserved you, and brought you where you are now ; over and above, God has left you a fair prince and two fair princesses, and God is still where He was, and we are both young enough. As

177

your Grace's wisdom is renowned through Christendom, you must now give proof of it by your manner of bearing this misfortune."

Then the King thanked her for her good comfort ; but when the Queen returned to her own chamber, the natural remembrance of her great loss smote so sorrowfully on her motherly heart that her people were forced to send for the King to comfort her. Then his Grace in great haste came, and with true gentle and faithful love smoothed her trouble, telling her what good counsel she had given him before, and " that if she could thank God for her dear son, he would do the same."*

On the 2nd February following (Candlemas Day), the Queen gave birth to her youngest child, Katherine, afterwards Lady Courtenay ; a week later, on her thirty-seventh birthday, Elisabeth of York's gentle spirit passed away. She was, to use her own words, " young enough in years," her great beauty enhanced rather than marred by a sweet autumnal grace. Of her last hours there remains no record : a MS. of the time mentions that her departing was " dolorous to the King as was ever heard of," and that he, " taking some of his servants with him, departed to a solitary place to pass his sor-

* " Lelandi Collectanes," Vol. V., p. 373.

row, and would that no man should speak to
him ; but (with characteristic thoughtfulness)
he sent Sir Charles Somerset and Sir Richard
Guilford to the Queen's servants with good
and kind words."

When the tolling of the great bell of St.
Paul's announced the Queen's decease to the
citizens of London all the people loudly bewailed her ; and when, after laying in state
many days at the Tower, her remains were
brought to Westminster Abbey, a great con-
course of citizens, clad in deep mourning,
voluntarily joined the funeral train, the procession of nobles being headed by the Queen's
oldest and truest friend, the guardian of her
girlhood, Lord Derby.   There is no mention
of the Countess of Richmond and Derby
having been present, but in an elegy composed for the occasion by Sir Thomas More,
in which, according to the custom of the
times, the deceased is made to take leave of
her beloved ones, Elisabeth addresses her
as

> My lord's worthy mother,
> Comfort your son, and be ye of good cheer,
> It booteth not for me to wail and cry,
> Pray for my soul, for lo! now here I lie.

Few Sovereigns, indeed few women, have
ever been so enthusiastically loved or so

deeply lamented as Elisabeth of York ; but it is curious to note that while all English historians unite in extolling her many virtues, her sweetness and her gentleness, her faithful submission to her husband, and her strong affection for her own kindred, they as unanimously allude disparagingly to her mental qualities, assuming that, though a lovable woman, she had been a somewhat weak and foolish one. Yet the Venetian Ambassador, who had special opportunities for forming an opinion, wrote confidentially to his Government that "the Queen of England was a noble and beautiful lady, endowed with great good sense and intelligence." She apparently exercised no political influence, but probably did not wish for it, as her time must have been fully occupied in the cares of her vast estates—for her husband, shortly after their marriage, settled on her the great inheritance of the House of York, which had been forfeited to the Crown, for her sole and personal use. So that though Henry VII. has frequently been accused of niggardliness towards his wife, she really had a very much larger income, and that entirely under her own control, than any Queen Consort of England has since enjoyed. And though the accounts of the Privy Purse show that

her personal expenses were small, Elisabeth
spent a great deal on the restoration of
Baynard Castle and the maintenance of its
beautiful gardens; also she was generous to
her sisters and gave much in charity.

After her daughter-in-law's death the
Countess of Richmond seems to have lived
for some time in great retirement at Colyweston; the only incident recorded of the
remainder of the year 1502 is her reception
to fraternity with the religious house of
Durham; the letter of reception written to
her by the Prior in Latin is given at length
in "Cooper's Memoir."

In the month of July following, King
Henry, attended by a great number of lords
and ladies, brought his eldest daughter, the
Princess Margaret, the affianced bride of the
King of Scotland, to Colyweston, that she
might take leave of her grandmother. After
a few days stay the Royal bride went on her
way with a brilliant escort to Scotland. The
Marquis of Dorset, the Earls of Derby and
Essex are said to have accompanied her a
part of the way; then, taking their leave they
kissed her, and returned to Colyweston,
where King Henry seems to have remained
for some weeks, perhaps to honour by his
presence the wedding of two ladies of his

mother's household, Elianor and Elizabeth Zouche, who were married within the month, the one to Sir John Melton, the other to Gerald, son and heir of the Earl of Kildare.

CHAPTER VIII.

THE COUNTESS OF RICHMOND became for the third time a widow on the 24th of July, 1504. Of the circumstances of the Earl of Derby's death no details are given. By his will he directs that the Countess shall peaceably enjoy all the lordships, manors, etc., assigned for her jointure, and that after her death her soul be prayed for by name in the Priory of Burscough, in Lancashire, to which he seems to have been a considerable benefactor.

In the portraits, of which several still exist, all taken when she was advanced in years, the Countess of Richmond is invariably represented in the dress of a nun. Not that she ever actually became one, but because in her third widowhood she made a vow of celibacy and obedience in all spiritual things before the Bishop of Rochester. At what precise date this vow was made does not appear, but it must have been within a year after Lord Derby's death, as Dr. Fisher was not raised to the episcopal dignity until 1505.

The following affectionate letter, addressed by Henry VII. to his mother, refers to Fisher's promotion:

" Madam,

"An I thought I should not offend you, which I will never do wilfully, I am well minded to promote your confessor, Master Fisher, to a bishopric: and I assure you, Madam, for none other cause but for the great and singular virtue that I know and see in him, as well in cunning (talent or knowledge) and natural wisdom, and specially for his good and virtuous living and conversation. And by the promotion of such a man, I know it should encourage many others to live virtuously, and to take such ways as he doth, which should be a good example to many others hereafter. Howbeit, without your pleasure known, I will not move him nor tempt him therein. And therefore I beseech you that I may know your mind and pleasure in that behalf, which shall be followed as much as God will give me grace. I have in my day promoted many a man unadvisedly, and I would now make some recompense to promote some good and virtuous men, which I doubt not should best please God, who ever preserve you in good health and long life."

The King's mother was no doubt pleased by the honour conferred on her confessor, and by her persuasion, as well as that of Dr. Fox, Bishop of Winchester, Fisher was induced to accept the good work of a bishopric. Some words of his on the subject of this promotion, though not written till many years later, may be quoted here, as they refer to his feelings towards his friend and patroness. He dedicated, in 1527, his work "On the Truth of Christ's Body and Blood in the Eucharist" (against Oelocampadius) to Fox, Bishop of Winchester—firstly because he was the founder of Corpus Christi College, Oxford, and if there were no truth in the doctrine of the Real Presence he would have given an empty title to his College ; and, secondly, for the reason that follows : " Ever since our first acquaintance, your Lordship had taken so affectionate an interest in me that I felt myself thereby impelled most ardently both to learning and virtue. You also recommended me to King Henry VII., who then, with the greatest prudence, held the reins of this realm, so that by the esteem he had for me from your frequent communications, and of his own mere notion, without any obsequiousness on my part, without the intercession of any, as he more than once declared to myself, he gave me the Bishopric of Rochester, of which I am now the unworthy occupant. There are many who believe that his mother, the Countess of Richmond and Derby, that noble and incomparable lady, dear to me by so many titles, obtained the bishopric for me by her prayers to her son. But the facts are entirely different, as your Lordship knows well, who was the King's most intimate counsellor, as you were also of the most illustrious King Henry VIII., who now by right of succession fills his father's throne, as long as your health allowed you to frequent the Court. I do not say this to diminish my debt of gratitude to this most excellent lady. My debts are indeed great. Were there no other besides the great and sincere love she bore me above others, as I know for a certainty, yet what favour could equal such love on the part of such a Princess? But besides her love, she was most munificent towards me. For though she conferred on me no ecclesiastical benefice, she had the desire, if it could be done, to enrich me, which she proved not by words only, but by deeds ; among other instances, when she was about to leave the world. However,

as I have spoken her praises in a funeral
oration, I will not pursue the subject here,
though she never could be praised too much.
This only I will add, that though she chose
me as her director, to hear her confessions
and guide her life, yet I gladly confess that
I learnt more from her great virtue than I
ever taught her."

These words of Fisher's suggest that to
those who have followed patiently this record of the incidents and environment of the
Countess of Richmond's career, some notice
of her personal and inner life may not be
unwelcome. The Bishop, in his "Mornynge
Remembrance," gives a vivid picture of her
mortification, devotion, and charity :

" In prayer every day at her uprising,
which commonly not long after five of the
clock, she began certain devotions ; and after
then, with one of her gentle women, the
Matins of Our Lady, which kept her till she
came to her closet, when, with her chaplain,
she said also the Office of the day, and after
that heard four or five Masses on her knees,
so continuing in her prayers and devotions
till the hour of dinner, which on eating days
was at ten of the clock, and on fasting days
eleven. After dinner, full truly she would
go to the stations of three altars ; daily her

dirges and commendations she would say, and her evensong before supper, besides many other prayers and psalters of David throughout the year; and at night, before she went to bed, she failed not to resort to her chapel, and there for a large quarter of an hour to occupy her devotions. Daily, when she was in health, she failed not to say the Crown of Our Lady, which, after the manner of Rome, containeth sixty and three *Aves*, and at every *Ave* to make a kneeling. As for meditation, she had divers books wherewith she would occupy herself when she was weary of prayer. As for fasting, albeit she was not bound,* by reason of her age and infirmities, yet the days that by the Church were appointed she kept them diligently and seriously, and especially in holy Lent she restrained her appetite to one meal of fish in the day, besides her own peculiar feasts of devotion, as St. Anthony, St. Mary Magdalen, St. Catherine, with others, and all throughout the year Friday and Saturday she full truly observed. As to hard clothes wearing, she had shirts and girdles of hair, which, when she was in

* In St. John's Treasury is a Bull of Pope Julius II., with leader Bulls attached, dated 4th May, 1504, granting an indulgence from fasting to Henry VII. and his mother, and to six persons named by each (" Cooper's Memoir," p. 248).

health, every week she failed not on certain days to wear."

The Bishop also tells that she was " houselled " nearly a dozen times in the year, that her tongue was much occupied in prayer, her feet in visiting holy places, her hands in giving alms to the poor. " Poor folk to the number of twelve she daily and nightly kept in her house, giving them lodging and drink and clothing, visiting them often, and in their sickness comforting them and administering to them with her own hands; and when it pleased God to call any of them out of this wicked world she would be present and see them depart, and so learn to die."

As to the nature of the frequent spiritual reading, of which the Bishop speaks, we can form a pretty good notion of it from the titles of the books already noticed. From the eager haste with which the Countess sent out two editions of the "Imitatio" in 1503, we see her appreciation of it, but also surmise that it had but recently come into her hands. But by common tradition her favourite author, and the one whose writings most influenced her spiritual life, was Walter Hylton. How she loved his " Scale of Perfection " the rude lines in Caxton's edition show :

This heavenly book, more precious than gold,
　Was lately directed with great humility,
For godly pleasure therein to behold,
　Unto the right noble Margaret, as ye see
The King's mother, of excellent bounty,
　Harry the Seventh, that Jesu him preserve.
This mighty Princess hath commanded me
　T' imprint this book, her grace for to deserve.

Inasmuch as a considerable portion of the
" Scale of Perfection " treats of the conquest
and complete mastery of the imagination, intellect, and will, as the sole foundation on which
the highest spiritual life can be built, and in-
dicates the methods of attaining thereto, the
author may be ranked among the mystics.
But, though he writes principally for recluses,
Hylton also addresses himself to persons
living active lives in the world ; and his book
has a certain historic value, because it fixes
an approximate date to the uprising of that
class of leisure and culture which counts for
so much in our present social order. In the
early feudal period, not only was the struggle
for existence intensely severe, but even
greater labour was required to keep possessions than to acquire them ; every acre of
land, owned whether by noble or serf, was
held only on the condition of service. " The
fact of possessing something implied that a
man or woman must work." But with the

reign of Edward I. a marked change begins :
the power of the executive increased ; despite many fluctuations, life and property became more secure ; and there grew up a class
which, as Hylton puts it, " could, if they
would, be free from such worldly business,
and have their sustenance without great soli-
citude, and whether in religion or secular
estate, having good abilities, may, if they
will, so dispose themselves as to come to
much grace."

To these he earnestly addresses himself,
warning them that it is perilous for souls not
to seek to make progress, recording St.
Gregory's well known allegory of Rachel and
Leah as foreshadowing the active and the
contemplative lives—not to contrast them, as
does Dante, but to combine them : " So
shalt thou do, according to the example of
Jacob, these two lives, active and contemplative, since God has called thee to the one and
to the other. By the one, thou shalt bring
forth the fruit of many good deeds in help of
thy Christian brethren ; by the other, thou
shalt become fair, clear sighted, and clean in
the Supreme Brightness, which is God, the
Beginning and End of all that is made. Not
neglecting thy children, thy servants, thy
tenants, and all thy Christian brethren, nor

letting them decay nor perish for want of
looking to. For thou must think that since
God has put thee into that estate of life it is
the very best for thee, and that thou canst
not do better than in performing all that
belongs to it in the very best manner, and
with all the willingness and gladness of mind
thou art able. This I say to thee, not as
though thou didst it not, but that thou
shouldest do it better, with more alacrity
and cheerfulness by reason of my writing ":
words which show that the Countess of Richmond, in undertaking to the utmost limit of
her life and strength so many and various
good works, and also in giving up what may
well seem to us so large a portion of her time
to prayer, was not following the impulses of
a naturally devout and energetic character,
but was deliberately shaping her life according to a definite plan, drawn up by a great
master in the spiritual life, suited to the
needs and circumstances of the time, to help
those situated as she was "to ascend by steps
unto the mountain of God."

Certainly, there is nothing in Hylton's
teaching different from that of the " Imitatio,"
only he puts it forth with less of what may
be called " distinction of thought and style,"
yet with a certain pathetic homeliness and

tenderness that is peculiarly his own, as in
his often-quoted allegory or likening of the
faithful soul to one who would go as a true
pilgrim to Jerusalem, but who, when he asks
the way, is told that he cannot arrive thither
without great pains and travail, without perils
from thieves and robbers and many other
hindrances so that few may reach it, and then
he is discouraged. To such a one Hylton
addresses himself, telling him that, nevertheless, there is one way, the which whosoever
taketh and holdeth to it, shall come to the
City of Jerusalem, and shall never lose his
life, nor be slain, nor die by default; though
he should often be robbed and well beaten
and suffer much pain in the going, yet his
life shall be safe. "Then," said the pilgrim,
"if I may have my life saved and come to
the place I covet, I care not what mischief I
suffer in going." To whom Hylton replies:
"If thou covet to come to this blessed sight
of very peace, and be a true pilgrim to
Jerusalem, though it so be that I was never
there, nevertheless I will as far forth as I can
set thee in the way towards it. If thou
wilt speed on thy way and make a good
journey, it behoveth thee to hold these
things in thy mind, Humility and Love.
Humility saith, 'I am nothing, I have

193

o

nothing.' Love saith, 'I covet nothing but one, and that is Jesus.' These two stirrings, well fastened with the minding of Jesus, make good music in the soul when they be cunningly struck upon with the finger of reason ; for the lower thou smitest with the one the higher soundeth the other. The less thou feelest that thou art through humility, the more thou covetest to have of Jesus through love. I mean not only that humility which a soul feeleth by the sight of his own sin, for though it is wholesome, yet it is boisterous, but that humility which a soul feeleth through grace, in the sight and beholding of the endless being, and the wonderful goodness of Jesus, and if thou canst not see it with thy spiritual eye, yet that thou believe it, for by this sight of Him, whether through faith or feeling, thou shalt esteem thyself as nothing, even if thou hadst never done any sin. Cast all behind thee and forget it, that thou mayest have this, which is the best of all. Just as a true pilgrim going to Jerusalem leaveth behind him house and land, wife and children, and maketh himself poor and base from all things that he hath, that he may go lightly and without letting. Right so, if thou wilt be a spiritual pilgrim thou shalt strip thyself naked of all thou hast, that are either good deeds or bad, and cast them all behind thee, that thou be so poor in thy own feeling that there be nothing of thy own working thou wilt willingly rest on, but ever desiring more grace and love and more of the spiritual presence of Jesus." And so on, through many pages and chapters, does Walter Hylton lead his pilgrim band, among whom, though separated by many years, but in unison of thought and feeling, the venerable Margaret might surely be counted.

If the question were asked what, in Catholic parlance, was the "favourite devotion" of the King's mother, the answer would be "to Our Lady of Pity," the desolate Mother holding in her arms the dead body of her Son which the Pieta, Michael Angelo's masterpiece in the Duomo of Florence, has made so familiar a type. There is an allusion to this in "Cooper's Memoir," and in each of her special editions of the "Imitatio" the picture recurs twice, though it has no connection with the letterpress, as if she had some foreboding that this bitterest of earthly sorrows was one day to be her portion likewise.

Still the habitual turn of her mind was towards action, rather than contemplation— as is shown by the warmth with which she entered into the project of a crusade against the Turks. Good old Fuller complacently testifies that in his opinion the pious lady was performing work more agreeable in the eyes of God when she endowed professorships in the two Universities. We, perhaps, living in the last decade of the nineteenth century, may think that to have freed Christian populations from Turkish domination had been a better work than even the founding of colleges. But in the Countess of Richmond zeal in one good work did not hinder the execution of another; of this woman it can indeed be said, " She hath done what she could."

We have seen how, as early as 1502, the Countess acted as mediatrix between the city and the University of Cambridge: two years later the latter body appealed confidently to her for help towards the completion of St. Mary's Church ; and in the same year, 1504, she made some stay in the city, probably in connection with the foundation of Christ's College. Previous to placing herself under Dr. Fisher's spiritual direction she had planned a magnificent chantry foundation for herself and her son at Westminster, and received from the King the necessary licence in mortmain. But Fisher judged it would be

more to the glory of God to devote her
bounty to the promotion of learning.*
To this the Countess agreed, but it was
necessary to gain Henry VII.'s approval
of the change, to which he willingly consented, and on the 1st of May, 1505, the
Countess re-founded God's House by the
title of Christ's College for a Master, twelve
Fellows, and forty-seven scholars. For their
maintenance she allotted twelve manors and
lands pertaining to them ; the King and the
Duke of Buckingham (the Countess' former
ward, now grown to manhood) likewise added
to the foundation by their benefactions, and
the statutes were framed by the foundress
in 1506 with somewhat minute but reasonable provisions. That she reserved for herself the use of certain chambers over those of
the Master shows how strong was the interest
she took in the College. Fuller has a quaint
anecdote that "the King's mother once, while
staying in the College to behold it while partly
built, and looking out of a window, saw the
Dean call a faulty scholar to correction, to
whom she said, *lente, lente* ('gently, gently')

* In the Register of St. John's College, it is expressly
said " By the counsel and persuasion of the said Reverend
Father the said Princess altered her mind from the said
foundation in the said ministering to the foundation of Christ
Church in the University " (" Cooper's Memoir," p. 158).

as accounting it better to mitigate his punishment than procure his pardon." It must be remembered that in those days University students were often mere boys, as they are now at the Scotch Universities.

But as the beneficent life of this noble woman—in earlier years so troubled by anxieties, losses, and bereavements — seemed drawing peacefully to its close, there came a final and crushing sorrow, one for which, as it reversed the order of nature, she had not prepared her soul.

From the first years of the century we find King Henry alluding to his impaired health, yet not apparently prevented from his usual avocations. After the death of Elisabeth had left him a widower, with only one male representative to continue the dynasty, there arose the question of a second marriage, which led to various negotiations with crowned heads. Bishop Stubbs is rather satirical about the young pretender of fifty looking out for a second wife, and making minute inquiries as to the age, stature, health, complexion, customs, conditions, and features of all the ladies who were thought eligible. Lord Bacon more indulgently says: "It ought to be interpreted that he meant to find all things in one woman, and so to settle his affections without ranging "; while a lady biographer credits him with unchanging constancy to the wife of his youth, on the plea that " though he talked of it, he never *did* marry any other woman."

Meanwhile, Henry had reached the twenty-second year of his reign and fifty-fourth of his age, when in the spring of 1508 his lungs were attacked, and he suffered from phthisis. Nevertheless, he continued to attend to business with as great diligence as when in health; in the summer he was better, and hunted much, still there were tokens that he felt his life slipping away. He had always been "a great almsgiver in secret; now he redoubled his benefactions, redeeming all debtors who were in prison for less than forty shillings, and hastening to finish his great foundation of the Savoy Hospital.* And hearing of the outcry the people made against the exactions of Empson and Dudley, "partly from devout people about him" (Fisher says of the Lady Margaret "that avarice was hateful to her, especially in her own kindred ") " and partly in public sermons,

* The Palace of the Savoy had been the residence of John of Gaunt ; Henry VII. converted it into a hospital and endowed it with lands sufficient for the relief of two hundred poor and afflicted persons. It was destroyed in the Great Fire of London, 1666.

the preachers doing their duty therein, he ordered restitution to be made to all whom his servants had defrauded."* Of Henry VII.'s last hours Bacon records "that in perfect memory, and a most blessed mind and in great calm, the King passed to a better world ;" while Fisher, who preached his funeral sermon, dwelt rather on his vivid and unswerving faith.

Many latter-day historians, both English and foreign, have asked the question why Henry VII.'s place is not in the foremost rank of English Sovereigns? The latest German authority on the age of the Tudors† says that "when the first Tudor ascended the English throne at the age of twenty-seven, a task lay before him which might well have frightened an older man, but the King showed himself equal to it : he had the happy gift of taking up first what was nearest his hand, and carrying it out with clear perception, calm judgment, and resolute will."

At any rate, Henry VII. had found his England weak and poor, drenched in blood, torn by faction, isolated in Europe : he left her rich, at peace at home and abroad, well-governed and well-contented, having

* Bacon's "History of Henry VII."

† "Konig H. VII.," Dr. W. Busch, kap. vii., p. 329 : Stutt-gardt, 1892.

a place in European councils second to none; he found an empty treasury and a mutilated coinage, he left his successor a reserve of nearly two millions, and a coinage which is still the delight of antiquaries and the glory of collectors. As to his personal character, "he was sober, temperate, and chaste, a lover and upholder of peace, but valiant and active in war; though frugal, he knew when and how to be generous; was affable, both well and fair-spoken; at Court festivities, though not given to feastings and frivolities, a princely and gentle spectator. As to his pleasures, there is no mention of them." With Henry VII., as with his three predecessors in name and title, even the fierce light which beats upon the throne has not revealed a single breach of the marriage law. "His times for good laws did excel; laws deep, not vulgar, as on the spur of the occasion; but out of providence for the future, to make his people still more and more happy."* During his reign the taxes and excise were confined strictly to superfluities; and his exactions, the one blot against his repute, were only levied on the rich (as is shown by the dilemma known as Morton's fork). This would tend to increase the wonder

* Bacon's " History of Henry VII."

that Henry VII. was not a popular Sovereign, only that from the days of Robin Hood to our own many persons have endeavoured to gain popularity by the apparently infallible method of taking from the rich in order to give to the poor, but few have been so successful as the genial outlaw. We have here, perhaps, the secret of Henry VII.'s lack of popularity : the nobility, though they helped him to his crown, had become estranged by his constant purpose of keeping down their strength and lessening their dignity, and could have had but little personal affection or enthusiasm for him. And it is quite certain that no English Sovereign misliked by the upper classes has ever been popular with the masses ; so strong is the solidarity that welds the unity of the nation.

Dr. Busch, in his " History of King Henry VII.," has described eloquently the imposing ceremonial with which the founder of the Tudor dynasty was interred. On the 8th of May his embalmed remains were conveyed from Richmond along the south bank of the Thames ; and in the gloom of evening, lit up by countless torches, the long procession passed in mournful state over London Bridge. In front were the sword-bearers, minstrels, the foreign merchants, and the chief officials of the Court in solemn array ; then came the Sheriffs and Aldermen, the dignitaries of the Church, and the legal dignitaries, while among them walked the friars and canons of the City churches, chanting solemnly. Next came all the peers on horseback (ranged), the spiritual lords on the right, the temporal lords on the left ; three knights carried the King's armour, and the Lord Mayor of London rode alone, immediately in front of the funeral car, which was drawn by seven horses, magnificently trapped, bearing the effigy of the deceased King, clothed in robes of state, under a canopy of cloth of gold, many lords and knights walking alongside. The Knights of the Garter followed ; after them came many officials carrying various insignia, the King's body-guard, and a number of private gentlemen ; the trade guilds and other corporate bodies closing the procession. After resting a night and a day at St. Paul's, where many Masses and Dirges were sung, while knights, priests, and heralds kept watch unceasingly, the procession moved on in the same order as before to Westminster Abbey, which for the solemn occasion had been lit up by a curious and costly light. Thence, on the following morn-

ing, after a long *Requiem*, rich offerings made
and a sermon preached, they bore King
Henry to the vault. Three prelates pro-
nounced the absolution, the Archbishop of
Canterbury threw earth on the coffin, the
Lord Treasurer and the Lord Chamberlain
broke their staves and threw them into the
vault, and the other state officials did the same.
The vault was then closed, and a pall of
cloth of gold spread over it. But the heralds
took their tabards from their shoulders, and,
hanging them on the railing round the
catafalque, cried out in lamentation : " The
very noble King Henry VII. is dead ! "

Though mortuary pageants are proverbially
as evanescent as funeral meats, all the
glory of the world is not so transitory.
Nigh four hundred years have passed, and
still there is on English ground no spot more
revered than the chapel which bears the
name of the seventh Henry. And if the
time prophesied by Macaulay should come,
when St. Paul's will serve only for a sketch-
ing-point, and Westminster's "tall towers of
talk" shall have crumbled, still will our
kindred from over the sea stand with uncovered heads in the glorious fane, that
is no unmeet sepulchre for the mighty dead,
who were their fathers' kings and ours.

In his will, made the year previous to his decease, Henry VII. appointed his beloved mother, the Countess of Richmond, one of his executors. Some writers allude to her as having been Regent of the kingdom during the few weeks that elapsed before the young King attained the age of eighteen. And she certainly guided his nomination of the new Privy Council. But this was probably at his own request, for of Henry VIII.'s respect and affection for his grandmother there is abundant testimony; however, in the discussions as to his marriage with Katherine of Aragon, which her trusted friend and adviser, Archbishop Warham, strenuously opposed, she took no part. Nor did the aged and stricken lady long survive the beloved son with whose good and evil fortunes her life had been almost wholly bound up; a few weeks after his death she was seized with her last and most painful illness, the agony of which, one who stood by her bedside tells us, put her faith and resignation to the fullest test. " Her hands, that were ever occupied in giving alms to the poor and needy, in dressing them when they were sick and ministering to them meat and drink, whose merciful and liberal hands had to endure the most painful cramps, which grievously vexed her and compelled her to cry out: 'O blessed Jesu, help me! O blessed Lady, succour me!' It was a matter of great pity; like a spear it pierced the hearts of all her true servants that were about her and made them cry also to Jesu for help and succour, with great abundance of tears. But specially when they saw death so haste upon her, and that she must needs depart from them, and they should forego so gentle a mistress, so tender a lady, then wept they marvellously; wept her ladies and kins-women, to whom she was full kind, wept her poor gentlewomen, whom she had loved so tenderly; wept her chamberers, to whom she was full dear; wept her chaplains and priests; wept her other true and faithful servants."

The best summary of the Countess of Richmond's character is that given by Bishop Fisher, in his "Mornynge Remembrance," or funeral sermon, which, according to the custom of the time, was preached at a solemn *Requiem* service, celebrated thirty days after her decease.

" She had in a manner all that is praisable in a woman, either in soul or body; she was of singular wisdom and a holding memory; a ready wit she had to conceive all things, albeit they were right dark. In favour, in words, in gesture, in every demeanour of herself, so great nobleness did appear that whatever she spoke or did, it marvellously became her.

" She was bounteous to every person of her knowledge or acquaintance. Avarice and covetousness she most hated, but specially in any one that belonged to her. She was also of singular easiness to be spoken to, and full courteous answer she would make to all that came unto her. Of marvellous gentleness she was unto all folk, but specially unto her own, whom she loved and trusted right tenderly. Unkind she would not be unto no creature, nor forgetful of any kindness or service done to her before —which is no little part of very nobleness. She was not vengeable nor cruel, but ready anon to forget and to forgive injuries done unto her, at the least desire made to her for the same. Merciful also and piteous she was unto such as were grieved or wrongfully troubled, and to them that were in poverty or sickness or any other misery. To God and to the Church full obedient and tractable, seeking His honour and pleasure full busily. A wariness of herself she always had to eschew everything that might dishonest any noble woman, or distaine her honour in any condition. Frivolous things, that were little to be regarded, she would let pass by; but the others that were of weight or substance, wherein she might profit, she would not let for any pain or labour to take in hand."

The Bishop goes on to advert in forcible terms on the loss the nation sustained by her death. " All England for her death hath cause for weeping; the poor creatures that were wont to receive her alms, to whom she always was piteous and most merciful; the students of both the Universities, to whom she was as a mother ; all the learned men of England, to whom she was a very patroness; all the virtuous and devout persons, to whom she was as a loving sister ; all the good religious men and women, to whom she was so often wont to visit and comfort; all good priests and clerics, to whom she was a true defendress ; all the noble men and women, to whom she was a mirror, an example of honour ; all the common people of this realm, for whom she was in their causes a common mediatrix, and took right great pleasure for them ; and generally the whole realm hath right cause to complain and to mourn her death."

Margaret Beaufort, Countess of Richmond, died on the 3rd July, 1509, in her sixty-ninth year. She was buried in Henry VII.'s Chapel in Westminster Abbey, in the south aisle of which her grandson, Henry VIII., erected a sumptuous tomb, said to be the work of the Florentine, Pietro Torriggiano. It is an altar monument of black marble and touchstone, each side divided by pilasters into three compartments. At the ends and at the sides are eight escutcheons within chaplets of laurel, surrounded by roses. On the top is her recumbent effigy, in her crown and robes of state, her head resting on cushions beneath a Gothic canopy, the feet are supported by a fawn, while on the ledge of the tomb is an inscription, composed by Erasmus:

Margaretae . Richmondiae . septimi . Henrici .
Matri . octavi . aviae . quae . stipendia . constituit .
Trib . hoc . coenobio . monachis . et . doctori .
Grammatices . apud . Wynborn . perq . Angliam .
Totam . divini . verbi . praeconi . duob . item .
Interpraetib . litterar . sacrar . alteri . Oxoniis .
Alteri . Cantabrigiae . ubi . collegia . duo . Christo .
Et . Ioanni . discipulo . eius . struxit . moritur .
An . Domini . M . D . IX . III . Kall . Julii .

APPENDIX.

Will of the Countess of Richmond.

THE COUNTESS OF RICHMOND'S will bears date 6th of January, 1508, but was not proved till more than three years after her decease.

After bequeathing her soul to Almighty God, to St. Mary the Virgin, and to the whole Court of Heaven, and directing her body should be buried in the Chapel of Henry VII. at Westminster, she gives directions as to the religious services to be celebrated for the repose of her soul in various churches and chapels and as to various legacies for Masses.

On the day of her death she wills that £133 6s. 8d., or more, be distributed among the poor; £200 were to be expended in clothes for her executors, servants, and other persons attending her funeral; her twelve poor old men and women at Hatfield to be maintained at her cost during their lives; her household kept together for a quarter of a year, and her old and serviceable household servants to be rewarded at Bishop Foxe's discretion. Then, after indicating many works of piety and charity to be helped out of her estate, and many kindly and valuable legacies to relations and friends, she completes her endowment of Christ's College, Cambridge, directing that the said College should be " perfectly furnished in all buildings, reparations, and garnishings of the same," and the Manor of Malton to be rebuilt at her cost, to serve as a house of residence in the country, whither the Society might resort to study in times of sickness at Cambridge, and a coffer with £100 provided for the College to spend as they need; while a codicil is devoted to the foundation of the College of St. John for fifty students, after the manner and form of other colleges at Cambridge, and furnished with books and all things necessary. Finally, all her plate, jewels, vestments, altar-clothes, books, hangings, and other necessaries belonging to her chapel and not otherwise bequeathed, to be divided between the two Colleges of Christ's and St. John's (Abridged from the full text given in "Cooper's Memoir").

Note I. to Chapter IV.

It is generally thought that Buckingham who, like Richmond, was descended from John, first Duke of Somerset, knew that the reservation, making the Beauforts incapable of inheriting the Crown, was not in the original Act legitimatising them, but an interlineation, made probably by Henry IV., and that Richmond had not this knowledge.

One reason given by Mr. Gairdner in support of this opinion is, that at the trial of Buckingham's son—the Duke of Buckingham in Henry VIII.'s time — it was deposed " that he (the Duke) had a certain writing, sealed with the

Great Seal, containing an Act of Parliament by which it was enacted that the Duke of Somerset, one of the King's noble progenitors, was legitimate ; and further, that the said Duke once said to Gilbert that he once had intended giving the writing to Henry VIII., but added he would not have done for £10,000 " (" Calendar of Bago al Decretis " in " Third Report of Deputy Keeper of Public Records," Ap. II., p. 231).

Note II. to Chapter IV.

Mr. Gairdner doubts Richard's second coronation. He thinks rather that he, his Queen and son, went in grand procession through the city of York with crowns on their heads ; but adds, " he is commonly said to have been crowned at York, and so one is apt to understand the words of the ' Croyland Chronicle' (" Richard III.," Gairdner, p. 567).

Note I. to Chapter VI.

On the subject of Sir William Stanley's arrest and guilt Mr. Gairdner remarks : " We have no new light, but some interesting notices of Henry VII.'s mode of dealing with treason in this and other cases. An anonymous informer, who seems to be speaking of the accusation against the Duke of Buckingham in Henry VIII.'s time, says :

" The King that dead is, whom God pardon ! would handle such a case circumspectly and with convenient diligence, yet not disclose it to the party or otherwise, by a great space after, but keep it to himself and always grope further. I am sure His Highness heard of the untrue mind and treason compassed against him by Sir William Stanley and divers other great men two or three years before he laid it to their charge."

However, Mr. Gairdner goes on to say, that while always awake to suspicion, and taking full note of everything he heard, Henry VII. never seems to have encouraged informers. Of this Mr. Gairdner gives instances, and sums up as his opinion : that it is not incredible to suppose that the arrest of Sir William Stanley was a measure intended to disconcert some special project which at that moment had gathered to a head, and that a curious document, lately brought to light, in which Perkin Warbeck makes over the kingdoms of Great Britain and Ireland to the Archduke Philip, dated about the time of Stanley's arrest, gives probability to this view (Gairdner's " Richard III.," pp. 352-3).